THE TARNISHED STAR

**Center Point
Large Print**

**This Large Print Book carries the
Seal of Approval of N.A.V.H.**

THE TARNISHED STAR

Lewis B. Patten

CENTER POINT PUBLISHING
THORNDIKE, MAINE

This Center Point Large Print edition
is published in the year 2007 by arrangement with
Golden West Literary Agency.

The text of this Large Print edition is unabridged. In other
aspects, this book may vary from the original edition. Printed in
Thailand. Set in 16-point Times New Roman type.

ISBN-10: 1-58547-945-4
ISBN-13: 978-1-58547-945-0

Library of Congress Cataloging-in-Publication Data

Patten, Lewis B.
    The Tarnished star / Lewis B. Patten.--Center Point large print ed.
        p. cm.
    ISBN-13: 978-1-58547-945-0 (lib. bdg. : alk. paper)
    1. Large type books. I. Title.

PS3566.A79T37 2007
813'.54--dc22

2006034319

1

There are high points in a man's life, and low ones, and times of terror and fear better forgotten but never quite forgotten however hard a man may try. Guilt and self-blame and cowardice live in us all, but so, also, do courage and triumph and pride. They make the high points and the low ones and these stand out in memory like the insistent words of the prompter in a play. They make possible recollection of the endless detail that make a man's life so full and so busy and rich.

Nineteen I was the day of the letter. Nineteen, and never shall I forget the blustery day, the sleet beating down nearly horizontally out of Colorado's high mountain peaks. Neither shall I forget the chill that touched me as, standing there miserably in the cheerless foyer of the tiny mountain post office, I read my father's letter.

It was brief and almost cold. *"Martin: Your mother died this morning at three."* It was signed formally: *"John C. Kelso."*

Brief and almost cold. The coldness, I knew, of a stunned man's grief. I had seen the bond between my father and mother too often to doubt it now.

It was the beginning, that letter. It was the thing that took me back across half a thousand miles to the wide, rolling land of New Mexico, to the waving grass, to the violence and hatred and death with which it was all destined to end.

I stepped out of the post office and stood for several moments on the icy boardwalk in front of it, scarcely feeling the bite of the sleet-laden wind. Then, almost dazedly, I mounted my horse and rode away from town, forgetting completely the things I had been sent to get.

Instead I was thinking of the things that had made me leave home. Never, back there, had I been Martin Kelso, an individual in myself. Instead I had been "John's boy," "Kelso's kid," "the sheriff's youngster." My father was a giant, whose name was a legend as far north as Wyoming and all the way to the Mexican border. I was young, with enough of him in me to demand more from life than living it out in my father's shadow.

I'd drifted. I'd gone from job to job, though neither because I couldn't do the work nor because I couldn't get along. It was something in me that drove me from place to place, some dissatisfaction with myself that even I did not fully understand.

The letter was six months old. Postmarked October 27th of the previous year. And this was April. It was covered with illegible scrawls in pencil—forwarding addresses, notations. It was worn and dirty and my father must have been thinking that I didn't even care enough to come.

Up into the high valley I rode and in at the gate through which I had drifted more than a month ago. I handed the letter to unshaven, grizzled old Dan O'Malley without saying more than, "I guess I got to quit, Mr. O'Malley. I got to start for home today."

He nodded and reached for the capacious black pocket-book he carried in one of his hip pockets. He opened it and stuck his gnarled hand in, coming up with a handful of coins. Wordless, he handed me my month's pay. And then he gave me the best short piece of advice I have ever received in my life. "Don't drift your life away, son. Find somethin' to sink your teeth into an' hold on hard. There's lot of old John in you for all you think there ain't."

"You know him?"

"Seen him several times. Heard a lot about him." He pulled a plug from his vest pocket and worried off a chew. "Hard thing, bein' a big man's son. Too hard for some. Maybe too hard for you."

I said, "I'll find out, Mr. O'Malley. I'm going to find out."

He nodded. "Good luck."

I went out to the bunkhouse and threw my things into my battered carpetbag. I caught and saddled my horse, the one father had given me when I went away. I tied the bag on behind, turned my collar up, mounted and rode away to the south. And as I rode, a peculiar uneasiness began to grow in me that nearly overshadowed my grief.

Unexplainable. Without cause or justification. But it stayed, like a coldness at the base of my spine. It stayed throughout the days that followed, throughout the long nights during which I sometimes lay sleepless and stared at the stars.

I dropped out of the high mountain country of Colorado, and the plain was turning green. The snow was gone at this elevation and streams ran bank full. The ground underfoot was soft with moisture and fragrant with awakening.

Calves cavorted around their mothers, their tails like banners in the air. Fawns lay motionless in the underbrush along the banks of streams, awaiting their foraging mothers' return. It was spring and the world was new again, but the icy feeling stayed at the base of my spine and uneasiness stayed in my troubled mind.

Across the endless plains, ever south. Across the Raton Pass into the vast, grassed land of New Mexico. Now, in spite of premonition and uneasiness, I was coming home and it was good and I could smile and stare ahead with eager eyes, searching out familiar landmarks and so measuring the distance that remained before I would arrive.

There came a day, a day when I saw the towering stone pile they called The Sentinel, and knew that now I was only hours away.

There were changes I could not help but notice as I rode along. There were squatter shacks at many of the springs and seeps and water holes. There were windmills along the horizon where before there had been nothing but the stark and lonely horizon itself.

And there were fences—fences around the squatter claims, and sometimes thirsty cattle standing listlessly outside.

The coldness at the base of my spine grew colder and the uneasiness grew in my mind. I knew the people who lived in this country, knew their temper and their pride. I knew the blood they had shed carving their cattle empires out of Comanche land in the early days. They were tough as the monstrous land itself, tougher than the tough Comanches from whom they had seized it for all their manners and their airs.

My father would be there in Rio de Oro, standing like a rock between those who had been his friends and these new ones who had come like sheep to inherit the land. Because my father was the law.

Except for him, I know that many of these squatter shacks would even now be nothing but piles of charred timbers and mud. Except for John Kelso many of the squatters would be dead.

I did not have to be told that the pressure would increase. It would grow and grow like that upon a dam as water builds up in the lake behind it. Until it became intolerable and the dam gave way. Or until . . .

I shook my head impatiently. I was speculating. I was guessing.

I passed The Sentinel several miles to the west. Though I was that far away I could still see the house of Mike McGann, headquarters of the McGann Land and Cattle Company, standing at its foot. I could see the other buildings clustered beneath the knoll on which it sat, like a town at the foot of a feudal castle.

Seeing the McGann house looking no different than it had half a hundred times before made me remember Sue McGann and I almost turned toward the place. But the need to see my father was stronger and I held my course.

9

In spite of that, my mind kept remembering Sue— the countless times she and I had raced across the waving grass, riding our horses with the reckless disregard for caution that is characteristic of the young. I remembered something else that made my face feel warm: sliding down one of the enormous haystacks a mile from the house, colliding violently at the bottom and rolling on. . . . I remembered how suddenly we had both stopped laughing, how we had looked long and hard into each other's startled eyes, how suddenly my arms were locked hard around her and my lips were seeking hers.

I chuckled softly to myself. Damn her. She'd meant for that to happen. And maybe more than that too. Only it hadn't happened because I'd got scared and broken away.

Slowly the McGann place fell behind until the only way I could place it was by The Sentinel, standing guard above it. The Sentinel diminished in size as I rode steadily along and I began to strain my eyes ahead for a glimpse of the town.

A haze hung over the land, a haze that was almost like fall. But I needed no clarity of air to know where Rio de Oro lay. Nor did I need to see the other large ranches to know exactly where they were.

McKetridge's Anchor rested against a long, gray escarpment a dozen miles to my right. Montour's Fleur de Lis was on my left and ahead. The Square D, Gus Dunn's, sprawled a dozen miles beyond the town.

The Big Four, they were sometimes called. They

dominated life in Rio de Oro and had for as long as I could remember. Among them they employed more than a hundred men and their families.

They controlled the politics of the town and county. They elected judges, elected the sheriff. The names of the members of the Board of County Commissioners read like a roll call—McGann, McKetridge, Dunn, Montour, Swope. Swope was Montour's son-in-law.

What did they think of the settler influx? I wondered. Or rather what were they doing about it? Something, I could be sure. They would not sit idly by while the homesteaders took over the land. They would not watch their regal way of life dissipated and blown away like smoke on a winter wind.

The town materialized before me, growing out of the haze almost magically, and except for thirty or forty canvas-topped wagons in the cottonwoods beside the river, this part of the country, at least, seemed unchanged.

Domingo Street, narrow as an alley, ran through the center of it like a snake in high grass. The Plaza was a bulge in Domingo Street like an undigested mouse that the snake had swallowed.

Santa Rosa Mission stood facing the Plaza and the courthouse on the far side of the square. The square itself was as bare as it had ever been, surrounded with unpainted benches. The carved stone fountain was dry and idle in its exact center.

But it was home and I knew every square inch of it. To right and left off the square other twisting streets led away, streets that a young man could walk at night and find whatever it was he sought—a woman, a drink, a fight.

You smelled Rio de Oro as you entered its streets. You smelled the pigs and chickens that roamed the back streets. You smelled the slaughterhouse at the edge of town and its towering piles of rotting bones and hides. You smelled the corrals, and the spicy Mexican food, and the liquor smell drifting out of the open doors of the saloons. You smelled expensive perfume briefly sometimes as a female member of one of the Big Four families passed. You smelled the cheap perfume of the prostitutes. . . .

Across the river and out beyond the town, on a hill so low it could scarcely be called a hill, I could see the cemetery. One of those stones marked the grave of my mother and she had been there half a year.

I rode down Domingo Street to the square. I had changed, I supposed, in the two years I had been away. I must have changed, for no one recognized me though I recognized many of them. Pablo Chavez, who ran the livery barn. Russ Lane, who worked for McGann. But I didn't stop and I didn't call out. I wanted to see my father first.

I turned the corner at the square, pulled up at the tie rail before the long, galleried adobe courthouse and swung to the ground. I looped my horse's reins around the rail.

One end of the thick-walled courthouse housed the jail and my father's office. I hurried along the time-worn puncheon walk and again I was struck by the lack of physical change in the town. Two years had passed, yet nothing visible seemed to have changed. The old sign, white with black letters, proclaimed that this was the sheriff's office. The heavy plank door stood ajar. I stepped into the cool, semidark interior.

My father sat behind his desk. And suddenly there was change in Rio de Oro beyond the intangible something I had noticed riding through it and surpassing any physical change that could have taken place.

John Kelso was unshaven. His shirt was soiled. And he was drunk.

I stopped as though I had run into a wall. I stared at him.

He lifted his hand and glanced at me. For an instant his face was blank. Then, slowly, recognition came.

I saw welcome, gladness, brief and soon over. After that I saw guilt, and immediately after that anger. He scowled and said, "By God, it took you long enough."

Wordless, I handed the letter across the desk. He didn't look at it. I said, "I got the letter a week ago. Look at it."

He lowered his glance and stared at the envelope. And I stared at him.

He was a big man, all bone and muscle, and his clothes hung on him with ill-fitting carelessness. His hair, graying now, was like a lion's mane. His brows were as thick and shaggy as his hair, and just as gray.

His hands were huge, gnarled and brown, and

incredibly strong. Their backs were covered with brown hair that showed no hint of gray. His face . . . The craggy strength of feature was unchanged, but something behind the face had changed—something in the eyes, in the set of his mouth. . . .

I said, "I wish I'd never left. If I hadn't—" I could feel my throat closing, could feel a burning behind my eyes. I said, "I'm sorry. God, I'm sorry!"

And suddenly he put his head down on the desk. With those huge, iron-hard fists he beat against its top until I thought he would never stop.

He straightened, his face white but scowling. Without looking at me he slammed open a drawer and took out a brown bottle. He uncorked it and put it to his mouth.

He drank, made a face, and still without looking at me, pushed the bottle toward me. He said, "Go on. Take one. It's the only thing that helps."

2

I remember that I was shocked. I remember staring at him as though I could not believe my eyes. I had never seen my father drink, although I'd known he occasionally took a drink with a friend. I'd smelled it on his breath when he came home at night.

But not in the morning. Not from the bottle and alone. Not one after another until he couldn't think straight.

I didn't know what to say. So I picked up the bottle and drank, and didn't let him see my eyes for fear they

14

would give away my thoughts.

Instead I turned my back, walked to the small, dirty window and stared outside. I said, "I've been drifting. I was up in Colorado when the letter caught up. How did it happen?"

He didn't reply immediately. I could feel his temper, his fury like a presence in the air of the stuffy little room. When he did speak, his voice was charged with it, thick, as though his throat were partly closed.

It roared like it sometimes had before I went away. "Fever! Lung fever! She'd have made it but for that stinkin' bunch of squatters out by The Sentinel. They had Doc out there and he was gone all night. Fixin' a man with blood poisoning from a wire cut on his foot. Son of a bitch lost the foot but that didn't help your mother none."

"How long was she sick?"

"Not long. Couple days, I guess. I was over on the other side of Fleur de Lis trackin' a bunch of stolen steers. I got home the evenin' . . ." He stopped, and I heard the sound of the bottle as he took another drink.

"I went for Doc right away when I saw how bad she was. When I found out he was gone I sent Pablo Chavez out to The Sentinel after him. Time he got back it was too damned late."

I remembered her suddenly and well as I stood staring out into the sun-washed street. A gentle woman she had been, whose gentleness had never been ruffled by my father's roaring voice. A woman who sat up at night when he was gone on a chase, who tatted or crocheted endlessly while her ears listened for and caught each small sound outside the house. Her face would be white, those nights, her mouth tightened a bit with the strain.

And when she heard him, heard his lusty yell from out behind the house—"Daisy! It's me!"—her eyes invariably brightened with tears of relief and joy. Then her small cambric handkerchief would come out and dry her eyes and when he entered she would look up at him, serene and dry-eyed and smiling now, and say, "Good morning, John. The coffee's on the stove. I'll get it for you as soon as you wash your dirty face."

He'd come across the room and pull her from her chair, the needlework forgotten and tumbled to the floor at her feet. He'd hug her and laugh and lift her up and sometimes he'd say in a voice only slightly lowered so that I wouldn't hear, "Coffee be damned! It's you I want. Come on to bed."

And they'd go and I'd hear them laughing and, later, talking, and thinking back now I knew that for all her gentle ways she had been strong and eager and full of life. She had met him halfway in all he asked of her. Losing her was like losing a part of himself, a part he could never do without, like his strong right arm, the one that was so lightning fast with a gun.

Now he drank to forget that she was gone and that he had been away when she needed him. I heard him choke and heard him say in a voice that was like a cry, "Why did she wait? Oh, God, why did she wait until I came home?"

16

But he knew the answer to that. She had always waited for him, because when he was gone she could think of nothing but his safety and the dangers he must face before he could return.

She had been my mother, and my throat was choked and my eyes burning with unshed tears. But I realized that she had never been to me what she had to him. His loss was like a red-hot knife that never cooled.

My voice sounded strange and not at all like my own. "I'd like to see her grave."

There was only silence behind me. It went on and on and at last I turned my head.

He sat like a statue at his desk, like a statue hewn of rough granite. His great hands were clenched into fists until the knuckles were white. His eyes were closed. Great pulsing veins stood out on his broad forehead beneath his leonine shock of hair.

Awed, I watched. Slowly the swelled veins went down. Slowly the color returned to his face. Slowly his granite mouth relaxed.

Last to loosen were his fists. He opened his eyes and looked at me and with a great, angry sweep of his arm he sent the bottle crashing to the floor.

I crossed the room and picked it up. I put it back on the desk but he didn't look at it.

Grief. I thought I had grieved for her. But my grief was puny compared to his. He had lived for her and would unhesitatingly have died for her. Now she was gone and he would have torn up the earth to bring her back. Only nothing he could do would bring her back.

17

Unable to change the fact of her death, he blamed and hated himself. He blamed and hated the homesteader who had lost his foot and in so doing had kept the doctor away from her. He hated all homesteaders because if they hadn't been here, Doc Steiner would have been in town when she needed him.

Almost dazedly he got to his feet. "All right, son. Let's go."

We went out and walked, side by side, through the twisting streets of Rio de Oro, passing as we did a dozen or more of the tired-looking farmers from the wagons down in the cottonwoods. They didn't look at us.

For all the liquor Father had consumed, he walked straight, but silently, with his face set and grim against the pain in his mind.

By occasionally glancing at him, I could see he was thinking of her. He was thinking of her, wanting nothing at all but to have her back.

Six months it had been. Six months since she died. If his pain was this great now, what must it have been immediately after he had buried her?

I tried to help him. "How have things been? I see a lot of squatter shacks around—and fences—and wagons down in the riverbed. How are the Big Four taking that?"

He turned his shaggy head and glared at me. Then, slowly, reason came to his eyes as he realized what I was trying to do. He growled, "The way you'd expect 'em to."

It was a cryptic reply and for some reason did not fully satisfy me. I said, "What are you going to do?"

I knew why his previous answer had failed to satisfy me. There was an evasiveness in his voice I had never heard there before. "Law says the squatters can file on a hundred and sixty acres. Law says the Big Four have got no right to their grazing land. How're they going to argue with that?"

I said, "Same way they argued with the Comanches in the early days."

He didn't answer. We crossed the near-dry river above the clustered wagons, climbed through the high grass toward the little knoll on which the cemetery sat.

I knew her grave at once—knew it by the flowers in the vase at its head, by the fresh newness of the granite headstone. It was raked and tended too, not like the others, all overgrown with weeds.

I could feel tears burning behind my eyes, could feel my throat choke up. She had understood me even if father hadn't. She had understood my need to go away. And she'd approved. I remembered her words to me the day I'd gone away. "He's too enormous, Mart. He's too darned big for you. If you stay you'll be overwhelmed. No matter how you try, you'll never measure up. Not here. It's in you to be like him, but not if you stay at home."

Her death hadn't changed anything as far as those unfortunate truths were concerned. But there had been other changes that she couldn't have anticipated. She hadn't known that she would die or that her death would be such an overwhelming blow to him. The old strength was in him still, but it was overshadowed by his grief. And I knew, in a moment of chilling premonition, that if he couldn't put aside his grief he would be destroyed.

We stood silently at the grave for several moments. Then he walked away, his face pale, his eyes almost cold. He walked across the grassy knoll past weathered wooden and granite headstones marking the final resting places of those who had gone in the years that were past. We walked to the far side of the knoll, stood knee deep in the blowing grass and stared southward over the rippling plain.

The horizon held its quota of windmills. Here and there a few posts, a few strands of barbed wire were visible. I said, "If the squatters homestead and fence all the water holes, what are the cattle going to do?"

"Die. Unless something else dies first. This ain't farmin' land. It can never be. But the squatters will drive the cattle out before they admit it ain't."

The statement held no conviction and he didn't look at me. "When're you leaving again?"

"I don't know. I'll stay awhile." I had the strangest feeling that he didn't want me to stay.

He said harshly, "Let's go back."

He walked past Mother's grave without looking at it. And marched almost angrily down the hill toward town.

I had to hurry to keep up. Watching his stiff-backed form ahead of me, I had the feeling that he was a stranger whom I didn't even know. What closeness had been between us before Mother's death was gone. It seemed as though we were two hostile strangers, fencing with words, each trying to find out what was in the other's mind.

I scoffed at the feeling. I had been away two years and a certain amount of strangeness was natural. But I couldn't entirely rid myself of it no matter how I scoffed.

Why had he said the squatters would drive the cattle out? It wasn't true and never could be true. Not while any members of the Big Four were still around.

I caught up with him at the edge of town. "Is the pressure getting bad?"

"What pressure? What the hell are you talking about?"

"Pressure from the Big Four. Pressure from the squatter group. You're right smack in the middle, aren't you?"

"I'll handle it. I always have."

"Last year was election year, wasn't it? How did you come out?"

He put a hand to the star pinned to his shirt. Mother had always polished it along with her silverware but it wasn't polished now. Except for the edges, where it occasionally got rubbed, it was tarnished nearly black. I don't know why the thought struck me just then but I remember wondering if its tarnished condition was symbolic. Then I realized I had no right even to think such a thing. Not when all I had to go on was this

21

vague, cold feeling of unease, an unexplained certainty that something was very wrong.

He said with flaring anger, "I got elected."

"By what kind of majority?" I heard myself probing. "As good as you used to get?"

"Damn it, what is this?"

"A question," I said quietly, "that it looks like you've already answered."

"So I didn't win hands down. What the hell does that prove? I made it. I'm still sheriff."

"But the homesteaders didn't vote for you. Why?" I wanted to stop but suddenly I couldn't because I was beginning to see a lot of things. "The next election. What happens then? There'll be twice as many homesteaders voting as there are now."

"Maybe there won't be any. Maybe they'll all be gone, damn their stinking souls to hell!"

The blazing hatred in his eyes startled me. I suddenly knew what the elusive strangeness had been that I noticed as we walked together through the town. It was the stillness that fell as we passed. It was the way people looked at him, or rather failed to look at him.

I asked, "That bunch camped down in the cottonwoods—are they coming or going?"

"Going, damn it. Why?"

I understood, then, the feeling of uneasiness that had troubled me. I understood the coldness that was in my spine. There was a fight going on here, a cold and terrible fight, for all that there seemed to be no fight at all.

And I could see something else—fear in the tough, hard eyes where I had never seen fear in my life before.

He was in the middle and knew it and he couldn't reconcile what he was doing, what he had done, with what he knew was right.

Yet there was another right as well—the right of those who had opened this land and fought and bled and died for it. John Kelso knew, as McGann and Dunn and Montour and McKetridge knew, that the influx of homesteaders, if not halted, would signal the beginning of the end. The end of a way of life, the end of free grass, of the power that so much land and so many cattle necessarily endows. The homesteaders were poor and had no real rights out here. Mostly they were people who had failed to succeed in the East. But they were locusts too, whose numbers had no end. And they had the backing of federal law.

I didn't know how he had discouraged the thirty or forty families camped down there in the riverbed. I didn't even know that he had. But they were leaving and they were sullen and afraid. That was enough for now. The Big Four had put the pressure on and my father had looked the other way. The star on his shirt was tarnished and the office it stood for was tarnished too.

I had been gone two years. I had been gone when I might have helped him bear my mother's loss. It wasn't my place to criticize or condemn him now. I didn't even know for sure that he was wrong. Right

23

and wrong have so many shadings that sometimes it is hard to tell the one from the other.

But I wasn't going to leave again. Whatever happened I was going to stay right here.

3

For now, I wanted to get away from him and think. I wanted to walk around the town and hear the talk, and I wanted to see some of my friends—the ones I could trust to tell me the truth.

My father's course, if I had guessed it right, was a dangerous one. It was far more dangerous than the one being pursued by the Dunns and the Montours and the McGanns. No one was going to blame them much for trying to hold onto the grass and water they needed to survive.

No, whatever blame there was would fall on John Kelso. He was the one who would have to bear the brunt of it all.

Intimidation wasn't going to work forever. Sooner or later the homesteaders would get together. They'd organize some opposition. And when they did the blood would flow.

I said, "I'm going to wash up. I'll come back at supper-time."

"Sure. The door's unlocked. Your things are still where you left 'em, though I doubt if they'll fit you now." He grinned at me in a valiant attempt to erase the words that had so nearly been a quarrel.

I said, "Thanks. But I doubt if I've grown that much."

I turned toward the door and stepped through to confront a scowling man I had never seen before on the gallery just outside. He bowled me aside roughly with a sweep of a hairy, muscular arm and stepped through the door into my father's office.

I was slammed against the adobe wall, not hard enough to hurt me but hard enough to make me mad. I rushed into the office behind the truculent stranger and reached for his shoulder to whirl him around.

Father's voice stopped me. "Get out of here, Shavano. Don't come bustin' in here with that look on your face or I'll throw you in a cell."

"Then throw me in a cell. Or better still, pull your goddam gun and shoot me down!"

Father said, "For Christ's sake, quit talkin' like a kid! What do you want?"

Shavano, a squat, burly man with thinning yellow hair and a week's growth of whiskers to match, stepped toward the desk. He flung a couple of scraps of paper on the desk. "There are two more of the reasons they're leaving. You're the sheriff. Do something! At least go down and talk to them!"

Father didn't do more than glance at the papers, so I stepped around Shavano and picked them up. He glared at me. "Who the hell is this?"

I didn't answer him and neither did Father. I was still hot under the collar from being shoved around and it wouldn't have taken much more pushing to

25

make me take it up. I looked at the papers. The first one said in large, printed letters: "A HUNDRED LITTLE HOMESTEADERS, SQUATTING ON THE LAND. ONE'S WIND-MILL TOPPLED AND SMASHED UPON THE SAND."

I frowned and read the other. "NINETY-NINE HOME-STEADERS FENCING WATER HOLES. ONE'S HOUSE BURNED DOWN AT NIGHT AND BACK EAST HE GOES."

I put the papers back on the desk. "Did you see these?"

He scowled. "I've seen some like 'em. Go on over home, Mart. I'll take care of this."

I knew I ought to do as I was told. I wasn't big enough to clash with my father and maybe this wasn't important enough for a clash. But right then I thought it was. Maybe I was trying to prove something myself. Maybe I wanted him to look bad because I'd always felt inferior to him and because I felt like a kid right now. Anyway I blurted, "The way you've been taking care of it up to now?"

His face darkened. His eyes were like stone. "Go on over home, Mart. Don't push. You ain't so big—"

"But what you can still take a strap to me? Is that what you meant to say?"

"Maybe, by God, it was!"

Shavano's truculence had cooled watching the two of us. I said, speaking to him for the first time, "How many more of these have there been?"

"More'n a dozen."

"And that's why those families are leaving?"

"Why else? They're farmers, not fightin' men. They're scared."

"What do the others say?"

"Same kind of thing." He dug in his pocket and came up with a handful of crumpled notes. He handed them to me wordlessly. The first one said: "HUNDRED AND TWELVE HOMESTEADERS, PLOWING UP THE GRASS. ONE'S HORSE DIED WITH A BULLET IN HIS ASS."

I read another. "A HUNDRED AND FIVE HOMESTEADERS, DIRTYING UP THE GROUND. ONE'S CATTLE STRAYED AWAY AND NEVER COULD BE FOUND."

I said, "Somebody's got a lousy idea of what's funny. Who wrote these things?"

Father shrugged. "Nobody knows who wrote 'em. It's just crank stuff. Some accident happens to one of these people and some nut makes a poem about it. That's all there is to it. Only Shavano claims it's an organized attempt to drive them out."

Shavano growled darkly, "What will you do when one of us gets murdered, sheriff? Call that an accident too?"

"Nobody has been hurt yet, have they?"

"Lewis and his family didn't miss it far when their house burned down. It wasn't no damn accident that their dog's throat got cut so he couldn't bark and wake 'em up."

Father struck the desk in front of him with a fist. His eyes were red, his face beginning to flush with rage. The veins stood out on his forehead almost as badly as they had a while ago.

I turned and went outside. I mounted and rode along Domingo Street until I came to our turnoff, and for several hundred yards I could hear him shouting.

27

There was no use in my staying there arguing with him. Things were strained enough between us already. I wondered if he knew who had written those notes. If he didn't, he could probably have made a pretty damned good guess.

So far the things that had been done weren't too deadly. A horse shot, some cattle driven away. A windmill pulled over and a shack set afire. But it wasn't in the things that had been done so far that the danger lay. That was in the threat implied by the wording of the notes. They were working down the list just as in the ditty "Ten Little Indian Boys." When they came to the stubborn ones who refused to be scared and refused to leave . . .

Shavano had asked my father point-blank what he would do when one of them was murdered, as one of them would surely be before it was over with. Father had refused to answer and by so doing had tacitly condoned the murder if and when it occurred.

I was halfway to our house when a gleaming black buggy whirled past. I caught a glimpse of Mike McGann at the reins, and of a woman beside him. Then dust obscured the rig.

It pulled to a halt fifty yards beyond me, whirled in the middle of the street and returned. I heard Mike's booming voice. "Mart! By God, it *is* you! How the hell are you, boy, and when did you get back?"

I dismounted, dropped the reins, walked through the dust to the rig. I put up a hand and felt it enveloped by Mike's enormous, calloused one.

I said, grinning, "Just did. And I'm fine, Mr. McGann. How are you?"

He returned my grin. "I'm fine and so is Sue, in case that was what you were goin' to ask me next." He glanced aside at the woman with him. "You ain't met Laura, son. Laura, this here's Mart Kelso, the sheriff's boy."

I switched my glance from Mike. And the impact as my eyes met hers was almost like a physical shock.

She reached across Mike and gave me a small white hand. I took it, my eyes never leaving hers.

She was older than I by several years. She was small enough for Mike to have encircled her waist with his two strong hands. She was dressed in black and there was a veil partway across her face. Her tongue came out and moistened her lips and her eyes clung tenaciously to mine.

There was something so personal in those warm brown eyes that I could feel my body heating up. I tried to tear my glance away and failed. I mumbled, "Pleased to meet you, ma'am."

"And I'm very pleased to meet you, Mart." The eyes were mocking now, challenging me, and yet it was a warm mockery without sting.

I pulled my glance away. Mike said, "You come out for supper tonight. Hear?"

I shook my head. "I'm having it with Pa."

"Tomorrow then. Sue will be counting on it. And so will Laura here—Mrs. McGann, that is." His eyes glinted a warning at me and I had the feeling that by correcting himself he was correcting me. But the feeling was soon gone because the glint in his eyes was gone and he seemed suddenly as embarrassed as a boy with a new girl.

He slapped the back of the buggy horse with the reins and the rig whirled on down the street. I stood looking after it and so did not miss Laura McGann's white face looking back as the rig turned the corner half a block away. I thought she was smiling, but I could not be sure.

I turned and walked toward the place where I'd left my horse, an excitement stirring in me that had not been there before. That woman—Laura. . . . There had been no mistaking the things that had been in her eyes for me.

I scowled and kicked a rock. Don't be a jackass, I told myself. She belongs to Mike McGann and you'd better not forget she does. It's safer to play with rattlesnakes than to play with her. Besides, she probably looks at every new man that way. If he took her up on it, she'd probably run like hell.

But however I scoffed, I couldn't drown the excitement she had raised.

I heard someone hurrying along behind me and swung my head. It was Shavano, plainly trying to catch up with me. I waited. He caught up, sweating and red-faced, and hauled to a stop.

He was dressed in heavy farmer shoes that were practically worn out. They were covered with mud, as were the lower legs of his big overalls. He wore no shirt, just his yellowed underwear beneath the over-alls. He wore a battered derby hat.

He said, "Looks like you're snortin' after that fancy piece just like all the rest of 'em. Play their game and maybe you can have a little of it too."

I could feel my face heating up and knew with acute embarrassment that it was getting red. And then I felt my anger rise, a flood that blotted out all caution, all thought, all reason. What he'd said had been exactly true and perhaps that was why I flared up so. I had, in my mind, been snorting after her. I'd been thinking . . .

His face was ugly, sneering. He said, "Nice little club you've got out here. Share the women but never share the land. What does it cost to join? I wouldn't mind a little—"

My fist lashed out and landed squarely on his sneering mouth. Lips split and gave and I felt the solid bite of his teeth beneath.

It had been an instinctive action, brought on by a fleeting mental image of that slight, black-clad woman in this dirty animal's arms.

He stumbled back, caught his balance and went into a half crouch. A hairy paw came up and swiped at his bleeding mouth.

He'd baited me into this; I could see that now. Because his eyes held a light of unholy glee. He couldn't touch my father directly but through me he could. And I had struck him first so there could be no legal charge, no matter how badly he mauled me. It was a cleverly con-ceived trap into which I had stepped like a stupid kid.

Now I'd have to go through with it, however it embarrassed my father and the cattlemen. I had no choice.

But I discovered that I didn't really mind. I had come up against something unexpected and confusing in my father, something that made me feel sick inside. It was easy to blame the homesteaders for the change in him, easy at this moment to hate them all just as I hated Shavano. I said, "Watch your dirty tongue," and waited for him to rush.

I didn't have to wait for long. He came at me the way a bull comes at a rival, head down, eyes red. For all his short stature, he was as solid and powerful as a boar.

I'd been in a fight or two, so it wasn't exactly new. And yet I realized that before this one ended one or both of us would be unconscious on the ground. He wasn't fighting me, nor I him. He was fighting the cattle interests, and the sheriff who was hand in glove with them. I was fighting all the homesteaders because if they hadn't come at all, my mother would probably still be alive and my father unchanged from the man I had known since I was old enough to walk.

Shavano was tough but he was also sly. I expected a head-on rush and sidestepped at what I believed to be the last moment. But his wasn't a blind, head-on rush. He changed direction as nimbly as a coyote and before I quite realized what had happened my whole chest felt numb and I was rolling in the street.

I had dirt in my eyes and I was stunned. I lay for an

instant there, then put my hands against the ground to raise myself.

His boot smashed into the side of my head and almost ended the fight right then. I went down for a second time and rolled, and my head was ringing wildly with a sound like a blacksmith makes beating out a horseshoe on an anvil.

I was nearly out. But that kick did one thing for me the rush had not. It raised my temper the same way the bellows raises the flame in a blacksmith's forge. I suddenly wanted to kill this dirty homesteader, this Shavano, more than I wanted anything else in the world.

I covered instinctively and caught his second kick on the shoulder instead of in the ribs, where it had been aimed. And as he drew back his heavy farmer shoe for a third kick, I rolled against him and brought him crashing to the ground.

And temper took over. Pure, blue-hot rage burned in my mind. He was trying to kill me or put me in bed for months. Only he was going to find that I had some of John Kelso's toughness in me for all that I had neither his years, his experience nor his uncanny skill with a gun.

I clawed along the dusty street toward him. I didn't even feel the kick I caught squarely in the mouth. I was going to kill him if I could and I'd never seen him before in my life until ten minutes ago.

4

Hot, powdery dust raised in clouds around us as we struggled there in the narrow street. No words came from our mouths, only gusts of expelled breath or animal grunts of pain and rage. I was bleeding from the mouth; my senses were numb from the vicious kick he had given me in the first few seconds of the fight.

But the animal instinct to survive remained, stronger in me than I had ever suspected it was. And I knew that this was no fight that could end with only minor damage inflicted. This was—this could be—a fight to the death.

He was a formidable adversary. Older than I, he was toughened by years of backbreaking toil. His shoulders were like those of a tough range bull. His arms were like a blacksmith's arms, his legs as tireless and powerful as the pistons of a steam thrashing machine.

Except for an occasional, brief glimpse, I did not see the crowd that collected. But I felt them. They watched with impassive faces but with some strange kind of pleasure showing behind their eyes, the same pleasure that showed in the eyes of a wolf pack waiting to tear the loser apart.

There was dust in my eyes, my nose, my mouth. There was blood on my knuckles from hitting his bloody mouth. Already two gaps showed in the even row of his upper front teeth.

Across the street we fought, and into an alleyway. I rushed him and bowled him against a fence, which gave with the impact of our bodies. Into a pigpen we went, scattering a sow and her litter of pigs into the alley, where they were immediately pursued by a crowd of screaming children until they disappeared from sight. I slipped and slid on the pig-fouled ground, but I kept struggling toward him, one hot need in my mind and heart—to tear him apart, to break him and break him again.

He tore the pig trough from the ground and whirled it around his head. He released it and it came across the pen at me, taking the legs out from under me with a crack that I was sure had broken both of them.

I sprawled forward and fell spread-eagled in the muddy pen. He rushed toward me, swinging a heavy shoe at my head.

I caught it and rolled away from him. He stumbled forward, fighting desperately to retain his footing, but he failed. Pivoted by the foot I still held, he fell like an undercut pine and struck his head against the fence.

The pain in my two legs was unbelievable. It snatched from my mind any sanity that might have remained. Still holding his foot, I struggled to my feet, realizing numbly that my legs could not be broken or I would have been totally unable to get up. I dragged him from the pen and back into the alley. I dropped the foot and waited for him to rise.

I didn't have to wait for long. He came roaring up, covered from head to foot with manure and mud, and rushed me blindly. This time there was no guile in his rush, no craftiness in his mind. I sidestepped his rush and put all the power I could muster into a wildly swinging right.

It struck the side of his head with a sodden crack as he went past. Pain shot from knuckles to shoulder. It felt as though my fist were broken but I didn't mind. It was good pain—the pain incident to inflicting injury upon this bleeding, incredibly filthy thing I fought. I followed him as he stumbled past me, and realized I was shuffling like a man in a daze.

He struck a mud-plastered adobe wall, hung against it for an instant, then turned himself around. With the wall supporting him, he waited.

I waded in blindly, my fists swinging like the arms of a windmill.

Toe to toe we slugged it out. I had no idea now of escaping injury to myself. I simply didn't care. If I had to absorb two blows to land one, I was satisfied with the trade. But I didn't have to absorb two blows to land one. I was landing most of them. For all his bull-like strength, he was weakening now and weakening fast.

Through the red haze of fury that enveloped my mind, I was surprised. I did not realize that we had been fighting for more than fifteen minutes. So stunned had I been by his initial kick that I had probably been fighting a good part of that time in a sort of walking unconsciousness.

Shavano began to slide down the wall. Now, every

time I struck him, his head, which had sagged forward, would slam back against the adobe wall with a crack. Then it would loll forward in time to absorb my next punch.

His eyes began to glaze, his lips to slacken. A drool of saliva ran from his mouth, reddened with blood, to mingle with the blood and pig manure on his face and chest. He slid suddenly all the way to the ground and my fist slammed into the wall where he had been.

I started to reach for him, nearly blinded by the pain in my hand. I stooped, and the world swam before my eyes. I pitched forward against the wall.

I fought to my feet and turned. My eyes were blurred, so blurred that I could not even make out individuals in the crowd. Only another wall were they, but a wall that opened to make way for me as I staggered toward the street.

I heard my father's roar of fury first, diminishing as he left me to stride into the alley where Shavano lay unconscious against the wall. Then I heard his laugh, increasing as he returned to me. He controlled his laughing long enough to choke, "You didn't come up smellin' like a rose! You smell exactly like a pig!"

He laughed uproariously, and peering owlishly at him and trying to focus my eyes, I saw tears streaming down his unshaven cheeks. I was so mad I took a swing at him, which he avoided with ease. But I was glad too. He was laughing and I hadn't seen him laugh since I'd returned. I doubted if he'd laughed since Mother died.

He said, "Come on," and we went down the street toward home with him leading my horse and me following sheepishly behind just as we had done so many times when I was a boy. Into the gate at our house and across the brick-paved courtyard beside the house to the pump.

He pumped a bucket of water and dumped it over my head. That revived me enough to enable me to strip the clothes from my body and after that he dumped several more buckets over me as I stood there naked and shivering in the thin spring sun. And all the time he was chuckling, "We'd just as well get us some pigs now. We got the name an' we'd just as well have the game."

I growled, "Shut up. Damn it, if you can't—"

He laughed again. "Come on in the house. You hurt?"

My temper was rising. "Sure I'm hurt! If you mean am I crippled, I'm not."

My eyes were working now. He stopped laughing but his face didn't lose its redness. Nor did his eyes lose the laughing twinkle they held.

Yet there was something else in them, something elusive and hard, at first, to put a name upon. I stopped being mad when I realized what it was. Pride. If Shavano had beat me down into the dirt he'd have succeeded in what he set out to do. Only it hadn't worked that way. The two years I'd spent drifting and working here and there had toughened me and given me a skill I'd never had before.

Shavano had meant to put Father in a bind by

beating me or crippling me. He'd wanted to make Father lose face through me. He'd meant to egg Father into arresting him.

And that's what would have happened if I'd lost. Already hating homesteaders, Father would have hated them more if Shavano had succeeded in putting me in bed.

Besides that, seeing John Kelso's son defeated would have put courage into the homesteader crowd. The myth of invincibility would be destroyed. Their resistance would stiffen.

A feeling of depression settled over me that was not caused entirely by the relaxation that follows the incredible tension of a fight. Already Father and the cowmen had me playing their game. Unwittingly I had struck a blow for them and I wasn't the least bit sure that was what I wanted to do.

I knew something else in that moment. Whether I wanted to or not, I would be a part of what happened here in the months to come. The violence would sweep me along on its crest until it either dumped me unhurt in some quiet eddy, or destroyed me with its force.

I could not avoid it and perhaps I didn't even want to avoid it. But I would have to pick my side and I already knew that would be the hardest thing I had ever done.

Hard, because I was my father's son. He had raised me to consider rich and poor equal under the law. From him, I suppose, I had inherited a sneaking sympathy for the underdog.

The Big Four had so much; the homesteaders possessed so little. But their coming was as inevitable as the passage of time. The homesteaders would build this land, would develop it as the cowmen never could. At least I thought they would. And with them would come civilization and progress. Wealth would pour from the land like honey from a horn.

Father carried water from the pump and filled the big wooden tub in the kitchen. I scrubbed until I stopped smelling the odor of pig manure. Then I got out, dried myself and dressed in the tight clothes father brought me from my room. I stumbled in there and collapsed on my bed. And went instantly to sleep.

My face felt puffy when I awoke, and the room was dark. I was stuck to the pillow with blood and it hurt when I pulled away. I got up, started to rub my eyes but stopped when I realized how puffy and swelled they were. I licked my lips and found them puffy too. I opened the door and came out into the kitchen.

Father sat at the table, cocked back in his chair against the wall. A middle-aged Mexican woman was cooking supper on the stove.

Father said, "Here he is, Francisca. That's Martin. Ain't he a hell of a lookin' thing?"

She clucked at him and crossed the kitchen, wiping her hands. She put both her arms around me and hugged me. "*Bueno*. Do not listen to the old one, Marteen. Sit down and eat." She stared into my face, clucking sympathetically. I pulled away in embarrassment, crossed to the table and sat down. I was stiff in every muscle but my depression was gone. Right now I felt a little proud of myself. I said. "How about Shavano? Is he all right?"

"Sure. His friends down in the river bottom carted him away. He's too damn mean to kill."

"Is he mean or—"

The grin faded from my father's face. "I'm not going to talk about him."

Tension was back between us, unspoken but there all the same. I wasn't going to get anything out of my father because every time I tried we got a little closer to a quarrel. And I didn't want to quarrel with him.

As far as law was concerned it was cut and dried anyway, and there wasn't much to talk about. The land belonged to the United States government. The government was giving it away to anyone who wanted it in 160-acre parcels. All they had to do was live on it and prove up on it. Maybe the Big Four would drive the homesteaders away for a while. But you don't buck Uncle Sam. Sooner or later there'd be troops in the area and the Big Four would have to let the home-steaders alone or take on the United States Army.

So we ate in silence while Francisca watched us with a worried expression on her swarthy, shining face.

A strain was building up and it wasn't what I wanted at all. Father didn't need me to tell him that what he was doing was wrong. He knew. Nor was he blind to the consequences.

I asked, "Who the hell is Shavano, anyway. I know

41

you said you didn't want to talk about him, but I want to know."

He scowled at me but he said, "He's their self-appointed leader. He's filed on Comanche Springs and fenced it off. But he doesn't want the land. He wants McGann to buy him off."

"For how much?"

"Oh, he hasn't made any definite offers yet. He can't because he hasn't proved up yet on his land. But he's talked enough so that everyone knows. He claims Comanche Springs will be worth twenty thousand dollars one of these days."

"And as soon as he proves up, he'll sell for that?"

"That's the general idea. Thing is, unless he can hold the homesteaders together, he knows he can't hang on that long. So he's doing his best to keep them from pulling stakes."

I remembered Comanche Springs. I'd been out there often enough. The place lay flat as the palm of your hand and had apparently at one time been the bed of a lake. The soil was rich and black, but more important than that, there was a spring there that ran even in the dryest years. McGann had dug it out and piped the water down into a series of troughs from which the cattle could drink. Now it was fenced, and it was the only water on that particular section of McGann's vast range. If he lost Comanche Springs he lost seventy or eighty sections of grazing land.

No wonder someone was putting the pressure on. And it wouldn't get any less.

I asked, "Didn't anyone foresee what was happening in time to do anything about it? Hell, McGann could have gotten some of his men to homestead his springs."

My father shrugged. "They waited too damn long. They didn't take the squatters seriously until it was too late. McGann eventually filed on his home place and he and the others have had their men file on one or two of the seeps. But the good springs were gone before they woke up to the fact that loss of the water would ruin them."

"Can't they buy the homesteaders out?"

"Not with Shavano around. Not with him talking twenty thousand dollars for his claim."

From where I sat it looked mighty cut and dried. It couldn't end in anything but a fight. The homesteaders were holding out for a price that the cattlemen simply couldn't pay. And the cowmen had to have the water or be ruined. The irresistible force against the immovable object. But something had to give, and would.

5

Francisca had just served me a piece of steaming-hot apple pie and refilled my coffee cup when I heard the drum of a horse's hoofs on the street in front of our house, heard them enter the courtyard and stop.

I lifted my head, listening, feeling a strange kind of dread. Then I heard a knocking on the kitchen door.

Francisca crossed the room and opened it. Sue

43

McGann stepped inside, her eyes finding mine instantly.

She had not changed much since I had seen her last. Her copper hair was wind-tossed and unruly, just as I had seen it so many times before. She wore a split riding skirt of green wool and a white shirt, a man's shirt that was embroidered around the pockets to give it a feminine touch.

She said, "Hello, Mart."

I put my napkin on the table and stood up. "Hello, Sue."

There was a strange expression in her eyes that reminded me of the one I'd seen there the day we'd slid down the haystack together and collided so violently at the bottom. Her lips pressed together and she said defiantly, "Is that all I get?"

I grinned at her. "I might do better if I was coaxed. I might not run this time."

Her face colored but her eyes didn't waver. They dared me to follow through. But the smile on her mouth was hesitant and she kept it there with obvious difficulty. She shot a glance at Francisca, then at my father.

I said, "I'll eat the pie later, Francisca."

She beamed. "*Sí*. There is a time for pie but this is not that time."

I crossed the room to Sue. "You look the same," I said, but it wasn't strictly true. She didn't look the same. There was a kind of recklessness in her eyes that hadn't been there before. There was something of

44

defiance in the set of her lovely mouth and that hadn't been there before either.

Wildness. That was it. But there was something else as well, something so humble in the way she looked at me. It embarrassed me.

I took her arm. "Come on out in the courtyard." I felt the muscles stiffen in her arm as I touched it.

I opened the door and let her go ahead of me. I closed the door behind. And suddenly her arms were around my neck; she was on tiptoe; her mouth was seeking mine.

I let her find it and felt my blood begin to pound the instant it did. My arms tightened convulsively around her.

Her body was small, warm, a woman's body for all its lack of size. My hand slid down to her waist, to the delightful curve of her back.

She uttered a small cry. "Mart! Mart! I've missed you so damn much! Why did you stay so long?"

I buried my face in her neck and her hands went up to run through my hair. I'd forgotten the lumps I'd taken from Shavano until her hand found the knot his boot had left on my head and stopped.

"Who have you been fighting with? Your face—this—"

"Shavano."

"I hope you beat the hell out of him."

I said, "I walked away," trying not to sound smug.

"And he didn't?"

"Huh uh."

45

She abandoned the subject of the fight as quickly as she had picked it up. "Mart, let's go somewhere . . ."

My heart beat a little faster and I could feel tremors in my hands. Her offer was pretty plain. I said, "All right."

We crossed the courtyard and walked out into the street. She hung closely to my left arm, taking great long strides to match mine and giggling as she did. She murmured, "It's so good . . . I really missed you, Mart. Did you ever think of me?"

"You were only fifteen when I left."

"Can't a man ever say what a woman wants to hear?"

I grinned. "I missed you like hell. Every time—"

"Never mind that."

She skipped along beside me. I headed toward the river, detoured around the homesteader encampment and went beyond. Her welcome had certainly been enthusiastic, I thought. I'd never realized . . .

But there had been signs, I remembered now, even before I'd left. The way I kept seeing her accidentally so many of the places I went. The invitations I got to dinner out at McGann's. The way she always tried to get me off alone. . . .

Nervousness began to plague me as we walked through the silent trees that lined the riverbank. In a minute now we'd stop. I wanted to stop. I wanted everything Sue had offered me. And yet . . .

I said hoarsely, "How long has Mike had Laura?"

She was clinging to my arm and I felt her fingers tighten.

46

I asked, "What's the matter? Don't you like her?"

"She's—" Her voice, saying that single word and stopping, was vitriolic. Then her fingers relaxed and she said, "He married her about six months ago in Chicago. Why shouldn't I like her?"

"I just thought—"

"Well, stop thinking. Stop talking about her too."

I said stubbornly, "She's got a way of looking at a man that—"

The fingers tightened harder this time but her voice was soft enough. "Oh. You've met her."

"This morning. I thought you knew. She was with Mike when I saw him."

"He didn't tell me that."

I don't know why, but I was certain she was lying. She knew I had met Laura. Then why not admit it?

She stopped and pulled her hand away from my arm. "I didn't come out here with you to talk about *her.*"

Her tone angered me and I said deliberately, "What did you come out for?"

Her arm swung and the flat of her hand collided fiercely with the side of my face, which was tender from the beating Shavano had given it. The blow hurt me and further raised my anger. I seized her arms and she kicked me in the shin. Then she began to struggle violently. When she couldn't break loose, she bit my arm.

I said, "Damn you!" but my anger was gone. She kicked my shin again and lost her balance, still struggling. I lost mine too and we tumbled to the ground.

47

I lay across her upper body, pinning her down. I found her mouth with mine and kissed her long and hard.

She stopped struggling and returned the kiss. And suddenly this was like that day out at The Sentinel in the fragrant hay. . . .

Her blouse had come undone and she found my hand with hers and placed it on one of her breasts. It was hot beneath my hand.

My lips were bruising, fierce. The fire mounted in me like a holocaust until nothing but Sue herself could have stopped me, and she was as fierce as I.

The river whispered softly and the wind sighed through the cottonwoods. Now and then a faint dog bark reached our ears from the direction of the town, or the shrill, sudden nicker of a horse.

There was peace at last, while the fire in us died to a gray bed of ash-covered coals. And Sue lay in my arms, warm as a kitten, soft as a featherbed. Her voice was the merest whisper. "*That's* what I come out here for."

"Hussy." My voice was sleepy, amused.

"With you I am. There's something about you that brings out the worst in me."

"Or maybe the best."

She lifted her head and brushed my lips with hers. She was silent for a long time after that and at last she said in a different voice, "Now maybe *she* won't get you."

"Who? What the hell are you talking about?"

"Laura. I knew you'd seen her. And I knew how she looked at you."

"I thought—"

"That she was Mike's wife? Do you think that makes any difference to her? If Mike knew . . . damn her, if he knew—"

"Knew what?"

"About those rides she takes. And the times she drives the buggy into town. Or about the times she walks down to the bunkhouse to see if she can find someone to saddle up her horse. It's a man, every time. A different one. And if Mike ever catches her . . . he'll kill her and the man too. He's old, Mart. And proud. And she's going to destroy him. Sometimes I think he knows, the way he pushes himself trying to please her. I know one thing. I want to kill her—I want to kill her before it's too late!"

"Maybe he won't catch her. Besides, it's not your—"

"Is that the way you feel about John Kelso?"

"No, but . . ." I raised my head. "How bad is it? How deep is he in?"

"Pretty deep, I guess. He owes—a lot of money—to Mike and McKetridge and Montour and Dunn too. For a while there was a poker game out at our house almost every night. He doesn't come any more, though."

"And you think that because he owes them money he's closing his eyes to the things they do?" There was outrage in my voice.

"I'm sorry, Mart. I'm just saying—"

I said, "What else?"

49

"They've promised him re-election. I heard them do that."

"They can't guarantee a damn thing unless they get rid of the homesteaders."

"You think they won't?"

"Who writes those damned poems?"

"Jesse Swope. He's the only one with that kind of sense of humor. But they work."

"Does Father know Swope is the one?"

"He knows. Everyone knows but the homesteaders."

I was silent for a long time. I was remembering Jesse Swope. I'd never liked him. He gave me the shivers, the way he watched a man with those pale-brown eyes. You always wondered what kind of twisted business was going on behind them.

We lay there in each other's arms, unmoving, each thinking our separate thoughts. At last she said, "Mike knows, Mart. I'm sure he does and that's what worries me. He knows what she's doing and it's tearing him apart inside. He's never admitted that he was old before, but he has to now. And it's aging him faster every day. Damn her!"

"Don't talk like that." I kissed her and felt my blood begin to heat again. I got up and pulled her to her feet. "Come on. I'm going to get out of here."

"Afraid of me, Mart?" she teased.

I grinned. "Who wouldn't be?"

Her voice suddenly wasn't teasing any more. "What I did—what we did—Mart, I was scared that she'd get you. I hope you don't think—well, that I come out on

50

the prairie with . . ." She stopped, in hopeless confusion. Then she said in a small, scared voice, "It sounds awful no matter how I say it."

I knew what she was trying to tell me. That I was the only one she'd ever let make love to her. I didn't know whether I believed her or not. But I guess I'd matured more than I'd realized in the last couple of years. Because it didn't seem to matter much. What did matter, to me at least, was what happened from now on.

I said, "I know what you're trying to say. And I believe you."

"No you don't. I can tell you don't."

"I do too."

She began to sniffle. "You don't either. You think—well, that I come out here with just anyone. You don't have any respect for me and I don't blame you, I guess. A girl that will do what I did—well, I guess no man can respect her."

I said, "Shut up. You're in quicksand and working yourself in deeper. I'll tell you something about men. There are two kinds. One kind chases a woman for the fun of the chase and when he catches her he doesn't want her any more."

"Are you . . . ?"

"No. I'm not like that. I'm the other kind. I've known you all my life. I know you're not a—well, I know you're nice. Maybe I found something out tonight. Maybe I found out I'm in love with you."

"Oh, Mart!" She was in my arms like a furry kitten, sobbing uncontrollably.

I said, "Come on. I'll take you home. If I keep you out all night Mike will make me marry you."

"Would that be so bad?"

"Terrible. I want to look the field over. I want to see if Laura's as good as—"

She kicked my shin savagely. I laughed at her. "Come on. I'll take you home."

We walked through the fragrant night. She clung to my arm with both hands and skipped along beside me. I caught myself wondering if she really had ever . . . I tried to put the thought away, but it kept coming back to plague me. It didn't matter, I told myself fiercely. But when I thought of her in someone else's arms I felt a fury rise in me.

We detoured the homesteader camp and entered the town. There were a few fires burning among the wagons, but I saw only one man and woman, squatting silently before the flames, staring into them. They must have heard us pass but they did not look up.

Why were they staying here in town? I wondered. If they were going home, why didn't they go?

Hope, I supposed. Shavano had talked to them and made them hope. Afraid to stay on their homestead claims, they were staying here and probably would remain here until their money was gone.

We walked silently up the quiet street until I reached home. Sue went to her horse and mounted, while I went to our little stable and saddled my own. I led him across the courtyard and stuck my head in the back door. "I'm going to take Sue home."

Father nodded, staring at me with penetrating eyes that I suddenly had difficulty meeting. Then I closed the door and mounted my waiting horse, wondering how much he could have guessed.

6

We rode out of town at a wild gallop, just as we so often had when we were kids, but there was an exhilaration in this that I had never felt before. Perhaps it was caused by this new, exciting feeling of intimacy and closeness.

I kept thinking how different Sue was from other women I had known. There was no feminine indirection in her at all and the lack of it was as refreshing as a cold drink on a hot day.

She must have ridden like the very devil to arrive when she did. She must have left immediately when Mike had told her I was back.

I grinned to myself. She'd wanted me and she'd come after me and she'd got what she wanted. Even so, there wasn't anything the least bit cheap about it. From what she'd said, she'd been in love with me a long, long time. And, I thought, I'd been in love with her too. Only I'd been too blind to see it.

Sue knew this country like she knew her own bedroom and she never bothered with roads. She just took off across country in the straightest, most direct route to wherever she wanted to go.

We rode until the horses were winded and then drew

them in to a walk. We were climbing the slope of a long bluff on the other side of which lay Cactus Springs.

I heard the shots and more faintly the yells as we scrambled our horses up through the sandstone rim and came out on top. I touched my spurs to my horse's sides and pounded across the table top of the bluff.

Cactus Springs was not the same as it had been when I went away. Before there had been nothing here but a fence around the springs themselves and a few hollowed logs into which the water ran. Now there was a shack, a corral and a flimsy-looking barn. The barn was afire, shooting flame and sparks thirty or forty feet into the air.

The light of the burning barn illuminated a circle nearly a quarter-mile across around the place.

Horsemen were clustered within that circle of light, and they were shooting at the shack.

As I watched, with Sue sitting her horse close beside me, I saw a man run from the house, gesticulating wildly with his arms, and shouting something which I couldn't hear.

One of the horsemen detached himself from the others. He galloped toward the man on the ground. When he was twenty-five or thirty feet away, his rope snaked out.

He galloped past the man, dallying the rope to the horn of his saddle. The man jumped like a rag doll when the horse hit the end of the rope. He thumped on the ground, then bobbed like a sled behind the galloping horse, raising a cloud of dust.

By then I was moving, maybe scared a little but more angry than scared. I spurred my horse recklessly down the rock-strewn, brushy slope, and could hear Sue coming along behind, calling my name almost frantically.

I didn't slow and I didn't turn my head. I thundered into the circle of light and headed for the man dragging the other as fast as I could go.

I heard a whoop. "It's Mart! Come on, boy, pitch in and help!"

I didn't turn my head. I reined hard over, deliberately crashing my horse into the one with the rope dallied to the horn.

The impact was frightening. I sailed over my horse's head, over the back of the other horse, and hit the ground rolling.

Both horses went down, a flying tangle of hoofs and rope. My wind was knocked from my lungs, but I fought to my feet and ran, fishing my knife from my pocket. I had to stop to open it but when I had it open I slashed the rope.

I shut the knife and dropped it in my pocket. The man who had been riding the other horse lay unconscious on the ground.

Sue had hauled her horse in. Now she sat looking at the scene unbelievingly. I stood spread-legged, staring at the bunched riders truculently.

One of them yelled, "It looks like Mart but it ain't. It's just another stinkin' damn sodbuster. Le's git 'im!"

I'd acted impulsively and without thinking, but I had

the satisfaction of knowing that I'd have done the same even if I'd had time to think it out.

They edged their horses toward me and I backed toward mine. I wasn't going to get caught on the ground if I could help it, but neither would I turn and run from them. As I edged away, I could feel my anger rising.

Dragging that homesteader had been a brutal thing from which it would take him weeks to recover. I had interfered and may have saved his life. But now—I could see it in their faces—they meant for me to take the homesteader's place on the end of the rope.

Worse, even, than the prospect of that were the things I saw in their faces as they edged their horses toward me. These were thirty-a-month cowpunchers. Some of them worked for McGann and some for Montour's Fleur de Lis. Some I didn't know but I'd gone to school with a couple of them.

Not one had what you might call a landed interest in all that was going on. Not one of them had anything to gain or lose.

You'd have thought their livelihoods, their homes, their very lives were at stake. Because their eyes burned with sudden hatred that was almost fanatical. Their faces were flushed. And in the eyes of a few was something very ugly, something that should never see the light of day and perhaps never would, for this kind always works best at night.

How far did I have to go? A dozen yards? Fifty? I didn't know. Except for that first lightning look to locate the animal, I hadn't turned my head because I hadn't dared. The instant I looked away from them, or turned to run, they'd be on me. They'd spur ahead and I'd be the one jumping at the end of a rope instead of the homesteader they'd had before.

This was the fungus that Father was allowing to grow and thrive. This was class hatred at its worst. A moment ago they'd hailed me enthusiastically as a friend. In a short half minute the friendship of years was gone and I had become their enemy. There could be no neutrals in the range war that was bound to come. You were for them or against them. You had to take your choice.

For a fleeting moment I wished I carried a gun and then, as fleetingly, was glad I didn't. If I had a gun I'd use it. I'd kill one of these men who had been my friends. And I'd probably be killed myself.

Right now I didn't give a damn who was right and who was wrong. This was about to touch me personally and I had discovered that it was myself I was worried about.

Sue broke the strain, unwittingly doing the worst possible thing she could have done. She cried indignantly, "Stop it! All of you!"

I was only a dozen yards from her. I could tell that by the closeness of her voice. And my horse was well this side of her. I'd seen that in the lightning glance I'd taken earlier.

I saw them surge ahead; I knew I'd never make it unless I turned and ran.

57

So I did turn. And I sprinted wildly for my horse.

I heard the rope sing out. I dodged aside like a running steer. But I dodged too late. The loop settled over my head.

I tried to stop, tried to keep from taking up the slack. I was an instant too late. I felt the rope snap taut, felt my feet leave the ground. And I heard their triumphant yells.

"Straighten 'im out! Show 'im which side he's really on!"

"Drag the bastard!"

Sue screamed. There was a sense of acceleration. The ground scraped me. I jumped and bumped at the end of the rope just as the homesteader had done.

I put my hands up over my head and got a grip on the rope. That way, my shoulders and arms protected my face and eyes. But however I tried to pull slack in the rope and gain my feet, I failed. The horse was going too fast.

I felt my clothing tear. I felt the burn of skin being scraped away. The endless bumping was like a dozen fists pummeling me all at once.

And dust. It was in my eyes, my nose, my mouth. I couldn't breathe without choking on it. I began to cough, and couldn't stop no matter how I tried.

Sound penetrated my consciousness. Yelling, exultant and triumphant. And screaming, outraged, terrified, infuriated. The screaming could only be coming from Sue. And then I heard a gunshot, sharp and loud, overriding all else.

I stopped being dragged. For an instant there was

utter and complete silence, utter and complete lack of motion. I seized the opportunity to drag myself to my feet. I stood there choked with dust, humped over, coughing and gasping for precious air.

I burned from head to foot. My clothes were in rags. Every muscle in my body screamed with tortured agony.

And my fury knew no bounds. I yanked the rope from around my body and flung it to the ground. I ran for the horse of the man who had been dragging me because there was a rifle sticking out of the boot. I yanked it out and levered a shell into it. I started to turn.

And I saw him as I did, lying spread-eagled on the ground not far from where I'd stopped. His chest, shirt—both were a welter of gleaming blood.

I looked around, appalled. The horsemen seemed to be almost in a daze. Their faces were gray now, their eyes wide and scared.

Sue sat her horse in an equal state of shock. She was trembling violently. As I watched, the rifle she was holding fell from her shaking hands and clattered on the ground.

That icy premonition had been justified. My coming home seemed to have touched off violence and death. First blood had been shed but I had a feeling it would not be the last.

But why did it have to be Sue? Oh, God, why did it have to be her?

I knew immediately what I had to do. There was nothing else *to* do. I faced the horsemen and said in a voice whose control surprised me, "I shot him. You hear? I got loose and snatched a rifle and shot him. I'll kill the man that tells a different story than that!"

I saw the relief touch their faces. Behind me I heard Sue cry out. I turned and looked at her.

She was completely out of hand, as close to hysteria as I had ever seen anybody get. But she kept shaking her head numbly. "No. No. I won't let you say—"

I crossed to her. I put up my arms and she slid off her horse into them. Then what little control she had of herself was gone. She sobbed, wildly and hysterically. She shook as though with a violent chill.

I held her so tight I thought I would crack her ribs. She needed that. She needed something to bring her back from her world of terror and shock. And I needed it too. I needed it because I was beginning to see the repercussions that would come out of this.

My own father would have to arrest me on a murder charge. The cowmen, those who had been my friends and companions for as long as I could remember, would do their best to see that I was hanged.

They might get the job done too. They owned the judges in the county. They'd *have* to get me hanged or the homesteaders would declare open season on cowmen trespassing on their claims.

I said, "Take care of him. And take Sue home. I'll go back to town and turn myself in."

Sue broke away from me. "No! I won't let you!"

I said implacably, "Take her home."

Sue cried, "I'll tell. I'll tell Father how it really was."

60

My voice was harsh. "Nobody will believe you. They'll think you're trying to protect me."

Her eyes were stunned as she stared at me. She knew what I said was true. She let herself be led away and helped to mount. She rode out with the men belonging at McGann's, and disappeared out of the circle of light from the dying fire.

I felt suddenly and terribly alone. The others, the men from Fleur de Lis, lifted their dead companion from the ground. I looked at his face. I didn't know him and supposed he had hired on after I had left.

They put him on his horse and rode away, leading his horse behind. His body flopped grotesquely from side to side with the movement of the horse.

And now I *was* alone. Except for the homesteader, still unconscious on the ground. Except for those in the house.

I walked over and stared down at him. He was a small man, about fifty, I supposed. He looked seventy lying there, his face gaunt and covered with dust and blood, his gray hair mussed and matted, his thin chest rising and falling slowly.

I knelt down and slid my arms under him. I lifted him and staggered toward the house.

The door opened as I did. I saw a frightened woman's face and the tear-streaked faces of two or three children behind her.

She held the door for me silently and I carried him in.

There were five children altogether, including a

baby lying on the table. All of them were dirty and their clothes were uniformly ragged.

The woman looked worn and beat. Her face was also streaked with tears. She was a plain woman, but she had good eyes and for some reason I couldn't name she reminded me faintly of my mother.

I said, "I don't think he's badly hurt. A few days in bed . . . Do you want me to have the doctor ride out?"

She shook her head. Her eyes clouded with tears and her chin began to tremble.

I laid him down on the bed, wondering as I did where all the children slept, because it was the only one. Then I made a hasty exit. I didn't know how much she had seen of what had happened in the yard. But whatever it was, I didn't think her word would carry too much weight. Not against mine and that of seven or eight cowpunchers. I hoped not, anyway.

Sue had probably saved my life. This was the very least I could do for Sue in return.

7

I closed the door behind me and crossed the yard wearily toward my horse.

I was beat, stiff in every muscle, sore and burning over a large area of my body from the dragging.

A scrap of paper blowing along the ground caught my eye and I picked it up. There was still enough light from the burning barn to read the words printed on it. "NINETY-SIX HOMESTEADERS CAMPED AROUND THE

WATER. ONE GOT DRUG TILL HE COULDN'T HARDLY TOTTER."

I grinned wryly. The description fitted me, anyway. I felt as though I'd never make it to my horse.

But as I mounted, my grin faded. It wasn't funny. Nothing was funny any more. The cowmen had given up weak measures and had resorted to personal violence. From there it was only a short step to murder.

The worst of it was, I knew they wouldn't draw the line short of murder. Not now. Not with one of their own men dead.

I wondered if it would have helped if I'd let Sue take the blame. I doubted it. Besides, there was one benefit to be gained from shouldering the blame that I hadn't thought about before.

Father was going to have to face realities now if he'd never faced them before. I had killed a cowman, at least as far as he and the rest of the country was concerned. That put me solidly on the side of the homesteaders whether I wanted to be there or not. And it put Father in a fix because now he would have to take a stand someplace.

I let my horse return to town at a walk. It hurt too bad when I let him trot and he was too worn out to run. The glow in the sky faded with distance behind me and I was alone on the black and silent plain.

Mother would have approved of what I had done. I knew. So, probably, would Father, if he were not so full of hate and grief. Whether they had rights here or not, whether they belonged or not, the homesteaders

63

were human beings. They were here. One right they did possess, and that was protection from violence. It was up to Father to provide that protection, up to me to supplement it if I could.

It was late when I arrived. The house was dark. I went inside and lighted a lamp. Then I went back out and stabled my horse.

Returning, I stirred the fire and moved the coffee forward on the stove. We'd be up most of the night and coffee was going to help.

I went to my father's room, the one he had shared with my mother. I put the lamp down and shook his shoulder.

He opened his eyes. He'd been drinking again. I could smell it on his breath and see it in his eyes.

Suddenly scared, I said, "Get up. I've got to talk to you."

"Not tonight." His voice was thick. "Go on to bed."

"It's important. I've just killed a man." I had been undecided whether I should tell him the truth or not. Now it startled me to realize that I had lost my trust in him. But the lie just slipped out.

And it woke him up. His eyes came fully open and he sat up suddenly. He swung his legs over the side of the bed and reached for his pants.

He stood up, shook his shaggy head as though to clear it. Then he roared, "That's a damn poor joke. What the hell's the matter with you? Are you drunk?"

I said, "I killed one of Montour's men. He was dragging me and I got loose and grabbed a gun."

He shook his head again, impatient with the fogginess liquor had left in his mind. But his eyes were clearing as he raised up from pulling on his boots. "Bring that damn lamp out in the kitchen. Maybe there's some coffee . . ."

I picked it up and followed him. He slammed open the cupboard door and grabbed two heavy china cups. He dumped black coffee from the pot into both. Then he handed one to me.

He gulped the cupful in two or three swallows, got up and poured some more. He stared at me with the old, penetrating look in his eyes.

It was hard to lie to him; it had always been hard to lie to him. But I had to bring it off now even if I'd never been able to before. He said, "All right now. Start at the beginning."

"I was taking Sue home. We cut across country and when we came to Cactus Springs we found the barn afire and a bunch of McGann and Fleur de Lis punchers in the yard. They roped the homesteader and were dragging him when I butted in. Then they started dragging me."

He didn't say anything, but he kept those penetrating eyes on me until I wanted to dig a hole and crawl into it. The hardest thing I had ever done was to meet them steadily, but I made it stick. I had to make him believe me. I had to!

I know now that I was a fool. A man is always a fool to mislead the law, to take on blame for something he didn't do. But I could still feel Sue's warmth, her eagerness in my arms. I had some quixotic notion it was my duty to protect her.

And perhaps it was. Time has a way of erasing facts. In time Sue would simply be known as a woman with a killing in her past. The circumstances would be forgotten. The story would assume a sordidness it had not originally possessed.

I said, "I managed to get loose from the loop. I was so damn mad I was out of my head, I guess. Anyhow, there was a horse standing there with a rifle in the boot. I snatched it out and shot."

"Who was the man?"

"I don't know."

"You don't know?" His voice was incredulous. "You mean you didn't even bother to find out?"

"I—" I lifted my eyes defiantly. "He was one of Montour's men—new since I went away." I felt myself beginning to get angry. "What the hell would you have done? He'd have dragged me to death if I hadn't got away. He'd have roped me again if I'd given him half a chance. If it wasn't self-defense I don't know what it was!"

I saw the worry touch his eyes as he realized what the repercussions were going to be. Montour and the other members of the Big Four, with the possible exception of McGann, would demand my arrest. If father refused, they might try and have him removed.

The homesteaders, used to distrusting him, would hardly rally to his support now. So he'd be a man alone, distrusted and even hated by both factions.

There was another complication that I hadn't foreseen. The homesteader group, led by Shavano, would demand that father arrest the Fleur de Lis and McGann punchers responsible for burning the barn and assaulting the homesteader out at Cactus Springs. They would demand that I identify the men. And if I did . . .

I felt a little sick inside. I hadn't liked what was happening to my father but neither had I wanted to get him into an impossible fix like this. Unwittingly I had touched the match to the fuse waiting so invitingly for it.

I said, "Will I have to go to jail?"

He stared at me as though the seriousness of what I had done was just dawning on him. He growled, "Not if I can help it. Come on. We'll see Judge Perkins and get you released on bond."

"You think that's best? I don't mind—"

"No son of mine is going to rot in jail for defending himself. I don't give a damn what the Big Four say. Or anyone else for that matter. Come on."

He grabbed his hat and marched on out the door. I followed. He tramped silently along the street with me hurrying behind trying to keep up. He had a way of making me feel just like a little kid. . . .

Suddenly I realized that feeling like a kid was my doing, not his. I'd go on feeling that way in his presence because by comparison that's exactly what I was . . . until I grew up enough to be my own man, to stand firmly and solidly on my own two feet. But I was trying. And maybe I was making a little progress too.

Judge Perkins' house was as out of place as a prostitute at an afternoon tea. It was a huge, three-story frame affair like some of the newly rich miners' homes that I'd seen up in Colorado. There was scrollwork around the eaves painted in different colors and three stained-glass windows in front, one on each floor.

It stood, like a counterpart of The Sentinel, on the highest ground in town. Judge Perkins was a pompous old goat who affected a fawn-colored broad-brimmed hat and a cut-away coat like Kentucky colonels are supposed to wear. But he'd never lost the nasal Yankee twang in his voice and for political reasons probably didn't want to lose it however he tried to ape the gentlemen of the South. He had his eyes on a seat in the United States Senate. I figured the country would be a lot better off if he stayed right where he was. It graveled me to be at his mercy now, because I'd never liked him and I guessed I never would.

Once when I was eleven I'd been caught in the hayloft with Nell Cameron and I'd had my hand up under her dress. Nell's mother had marched me home with an iron grip on my right ear and I remembered that I'd felt exactly the same way then as I did right now. Father marched up the walk and twisted the bell so hard I thought he'd break it off.

We waited. It seemed like we waited forever. Then I saw a flicker of light faintly through the stained-glass panel of the door and a few moments later heard the latch.

Father said, "I want to see Judge Perkins. Tell him it's urgent."

"Yassuh. Come in, suh, an' wait in the parlor."

We went in and the colored man shuffled away, his slippers slapping softly as he went. Father went around and lighted several lamps. I sat hunched miserably in one of the huge brocaded chairs, ragged, dirty and beat.

I stared numbly across at Father. There was more of the old John Kelso in him tonight than I'd seen since I'd come home. He was unshaven and his eyes were red. His great hands trembled slightly. But the old set was back in his jaw and his eyes were as hard as pieces of stone.

Judge Perkins came into the room. His white hair was carefully combed and he was dressed in a handsome red bathrobe and matching slippers. He said, after clearing his throat deliberately and pompously, "John! What is it! And Martin! Good to see you back, boy. Good to see you back. My deepest sympathy. . . ." They were words and only words, as empty as the man speaking them. All the time he was staring at the condition of my clothes and face with unconcealed disapproval.

Father said without preamble, "I'm charging Martin here with homicide. I want you to set his bond so that I can release him."

"Who—what—?" Perkins stuttered confusedly.

"A Fleur de Lis hand. They were dragging Satterlee out at Cactus Springs. Mart was taking Sue McGann home and interfered. So they started dragging Mart. Only he got loose and got a gun. He shot one of them. It was self-defense, plain and simple, but he'll have to go to trial just the same. I want a clear-cut acquittal by a court."

You could see Judge Perkins' mind working, weighing this for possible advantage to himself. He said, "The Big Four—"

"The Big Four be damned!"

"I don't know . . ."

Father got up. He walked over and yanked the judge to his feet. "You'd better know, and fast. You set the bond and set it now!"

Perkins' face flushed angrily. His eyes snapped. "Don't you talk to me like that! I'm—"

Father looked long and hard into the judge's eyes. Perkins seemed to wilt. He said, "All right, John. All right. No need to get worked up. I'll set the bond at five hundred dollars."

Father released him. "Fix up the papers."

Perkins crossed the room to a desk, shaking his head. "This is terrible, John! It will blow the country wide open."

"Then let it blow. Maybe it's time it did."

But there was something—of worry, perhaps of outright fear—behind his hard old eyes. He would buck the Big Four for me, but he knew it wouldn't be easy. And for some reason he was afraid.

8

If I slept at all that night, it was only in snatches, and even these short snatches must have been disturbed by uneasy, twisted dreams. The state of being awake and that of being asleep seemed to blend until I didn't know one from the other, the wild fantasy of dreaming from the equally wild fantasy of reality.

Endless though it seemed, the night did pass and morning came. I got up at almost the same instant Father did and for the first few minutes we avoided each other's eyes while we gathered and arranged our disorganized thoughts.

I remembered the nightmarish quality of last night's happenings—the killing out at Cactus Springs, the midnight visit to Judge Perkins' house.

This morning there would be hell to pay. The Big Four would come swarming into town itching for a fight and howling for my blood. Regardless of how they felt about the killing, they knew they couldn't afford to let it go unavenged.

I asked, "How long do you think it'll take 'em to get here?"

"Who?" He asked the question but he knew what I meant.

"The Big Four. Who else? They sure as hell won't let this pass."

He frowned. "No. I don't suppose they will."

"What do you think they'll do?"

71

Uncertainty and worry were brief clouds passing across his seamed and unshaven face. They were gone then, and his jaw hardened and anger touched his eyes. "Nothin'. They'll blow and they'll yell but it won't do 'em any good."

I nodded and we went out to wash, returning afterward to sit silently at the breakfast table while an equally silent and worried Francisca served us.

I realized that I was straining my ears, listening for their approach. In a way I was glad that the time for decision was here. I was glad my action had forced Father to quit shilly-shallying and take his stand. Yet I was sorry too because I knew taking such a stand might ruin him or cause his death, and for that I would be responsible.

The morning noises of the town drifted into the courtyard and through the open door, but the sounds of rapidly approaching hoofs did not come. We finished our breakfast, got up and went out into the morning sunlight. Father rolled a smoke with a wheat-straw paper and a sack of tobacco, handed me the makings when he had finished. I rolled one for myself and struck a match. His eyes avoided mine as I touched the flame to his cigarette.

We walked toward the thick-walled adobe court-house and the office and jail at one end of it.

My body ached from the fight with Shavano and burned from the dragging last night at Cactus Springs. One of my legs must have been badly wrenched because I could scarcely walk on it without limping.

We reached the office at seven and Father unlocked the door. The sun was a third of the distance up the sky and already growing hot. Father sat down in his swivel chair and lighted a cigar. He sat unmoving, staring at the wall across the room from his desk.

I paced back and forth in front of the window, occasionally stopping to peer outside. The strain of waiting increased, but neither of us spoke.

Half an hour passed before we heard it at last, the distant drum of many horses' hoofs against the hard-packed dirt streets of the untidy town. It increased rapidly in volume and then I saw them come thundering around the corner across the square.

There were five and I could have named four without even looking. Montour. McGann. Dunn. McKetridge. The fifth would have to be Swope, Montour's son-in-law.

They pulled up, plunging, before the courthouse. I glanced briefly at each member of the Big Four, then at Swope.

He was tall—as tall as I. He was scarcely lighter than I but seemed so because he was older, and bonier, and because his clothes hung more loosely from his body.

He wore dusty Texas boots with great cartwheel spurs and straight, thin-shanked woolen pants. He wore a spotless white shirt that contrasted sharply with both his shapeless hat and dusty pants.

Sagging against one thigh was a walnut-handled gun in a cutaway holster. And from the bottom of the holster a thong ran around his leg just above the knee to hold the holster down as he drew the gun.

They dismounted deliberately and tied their lathered horses to the rail. They ducked under the rail, one by one, and without speaking came across the uneven puncheon walk to the door.

It opened. McGann came in first, followed by the other four. McGann stared at me and scowled.

Swope spoke first, in an angry, intemperate tone. "What the hell's he doing out of jail? He killed a man last night!"

Father's great head came around and his eyes fixed themselves unwinkingly on Swope. But he didn't speak.

McGann growled, "Shut up, Jess."

Swope's face flushed. His lips thinned out and his eyes narrowed dangerously. Without looking at McGann he muttered, "By God, Link was a friend of mine! If you think—"

McGann repeated ominously, "I said shut up!"

Swope put his pale-brown eyes on McGann. "Someday I'm going to kill you, old man."

McGann's hand swung. It collided violently with the side of Swope's face. The man staggered aside, his hand streaking for his gun.

Father stuck out a foot. Swope tripped over it and sprawled on the floor. His gun came out, and up. Father kicked it violently out of his hand.

I have never seen a look more murderous than the one Swope divided between my father and McGann.

He got to his feet deliberately and shuffled across the room to pick up his gun. He shoved it back into its holster and returned.

McGann said, "Put Martin in jail, John."

"No. He's out on bail."

McGann's voice remained patient. "He's your son, John. You must realize how it's going to look if he's free on bail. The damned homesteaders will make a hero out of him. They'll figure you approve of what he's done."

Father stared straight at McGann. "Maybe I do."

"You don't mean that, John. He acted hastily and foolishly and you know it as well as I do. They wasn't goin' to kill that sodbuster. They'd have quit just as quick whether Martin interfered or not."

"And they might have killed the man."

McGann's shoulders lifted in the slightest of shrugs.

My father's voice took on a new edge. "I'll tell you right now. I'll tell you all. I draw the line at murder. I'll arrest a killer even if I have to come into your homes for him."

I stood there listening like a bump on a log, growing angrier each moment that I did. It infuriated me to have them stand here discussing me, in my presence, without a word to me about it.

I tried to hold my temper and failed. I shoved Montour out of the way and stepped into the middle of the group. I said, "What am I, a kid or something? I've got something to say about what happens to me. And I'm damn sure not going to apologize for what happened last night—not to you or anybody else."

Swope stepped close to me. There was threat in his pale eyes and a growing sneer on his thin mouth. Before he could speak, I put my hand in the middle of his chest and shoved.

He staggered back and for the second time in as many minutes, he sprawled awkwardly to the floor.

It was as though the actors in a drama forgot they had played a scene and therefore played it over. His hand groped for his gun and he yanked it out.

Suddenly the little patience that remained in me was gone. Anger and outrage took over completely.

I forgot to be concerned that Swope might blow my damn-fool head off before I could get to him. I crossed the room in a couple of quick strides and slammed my heel down on his wrist, grinding as I did.

The gun slipped from his fingers. He howled with the pain. He rolled against my legs and brought me down on top of him.

Fierce satisfaction was the only thing I felt. He kneed me in the groin and pain shot up through my belly. He elbowed me as he tried to rise and smashed my lips against my teeth. He tried to crawl across me and get his gun.

I sat up and chopped savagely at the back of his neck. The blow struck squarely and he went limp.

I struggled to my feet, seized him by the boots and dragged him out the door.

His head bumped solidly against the puncheon walk outside. He was struggling already, coming to.

I stepped back to wait, a corner of my eye catching

the forms of McGann, Montour, McKetridge and Dunn crowding out the door. Another form stayed in it, that of my father, and he did not attempt to interfere.

Swope got to his hands and knees. He shook his hanging head. He raised it slightly, saw my boots, then let his glance travel upward until it reached my face.

He began to curse me, using every profanity and obscenity I had ever heard. I wanted to kick him in the mouth but I didn't want this to end that quickly. So I crossed the walk to him and cuffed him squarely on the mouth with the back of my hand.

It knocked him sprawling but he came up this time like a cat. I said nastily, "No guns this time. Maybe you won't do so good with just your hands and feet."

I saw his glance go to the gun I had strapped on early this morning. If he could get his hands on it as we were grappling together . . . I grinned mockingly at him as I lifted it from the holster and tossed it to my father. He caught it deftly by the barrel.

While I was still off guard from the toss, Swope rushed. He lunged at me with his arms windmilling and caught me on the side of the neck with one wildly swinging fist.

I heard, or felt, the crack of my neck. I staggered aside, stunned by the blow.

He followed, a nastily triumphant grin on his face. I stepped aside and he rushed past toward the solid wall of adobe behind me. I swung at him as he passed, and connected, and drove him with even greater momentum toward the wall.

He struck it with a thud, his shoulder striking first. When he turned, his back to it, I was ready for him. The stunning effect of the blow on my neck was gone. I was alert, cold, ready now to do what I had always wanted to do to Swope.

I took a slow step toward him—another. I could see decision flicker in his eyes and he lunged toward me again.

Before he had more than cleared the wall I lashed out, with short, savage, cutting blows, never giving him a chance to recover his balance. Each blow slammed his head back against the adobe wall. Each left its bruising mark on his face.

Something came over me that I had never experienced before. I no longer seemed to be fighting a man. Instead it was as though I were trying to kill a snake that would not die. Each blow made him writhe but he refused to die and be still.

There was blood on my fists. Swope's skin was the pasty color of a reptile's belly except for the places where blood had splotched it. I heard voices, seeming to come from far away, but I didn't stop. I wouldn't have stopped even had I understood the words those voices made.

Hands clawed at me and I turned to fight them off. Swope recovered and staggered away from the wall.

My own sight was blurred with fury. But I saw him close with a dimly seen figure and step away, now holding a gun.

Orange flame and black powder smoke shot from

the gun in his hand. I felt a burning, searing pain along the right side of my body, over the ribs.

The pain was nothing compared to the realization that he had wounded me. That infuriated me. I broke away from the hands, holding me and stumbled toward Swope.

My own unsteadiness told me I had not escaped punishment at the gunman's hands. But I was still on my feet, still strong enough. . . .

I reached him as the gun discharged a second time. This bullet made a buzzing noise and stirred my hair as it passed close to my right ear.

Then I had my hands on him. I wrenched the gun from his fingers. Palming it, I struck him on the side of the head.

He fell away. I staggered forward to fall on top of him. I drew back the gun for a second blow.

It was wrenched from my hands. I heard my father's booming voice, felt his enormous, powerful hands. "Enough, Mart. Enough. I don't want to have to post bail again—not for the likes of him."

He helped me to my feet. I stared down at Swope, unconscious on the ground. There was utter silence in the street. The few townspeople who had gathered to watch began to drift away, muttering softly among themselves, partly in English, partly in Spanish.

Father said, "Go home, Mart, and get cleaned up."

I nodded dumbly, turned and stumbled away. Behind me the silence was complete. I had gone half a block before I realized why.

9

As soon as I did realize why it had been so quiet back there, I stopped. I stood swaying in the sun for several moments. They had not talked because they wanted me gone before they did. And that meant that neither my father nor the Big Four wanted me to hear what was said.

I turned. I was standing beside a narrow gate leading to a small courtyard. Inside I could see a well.

I walked in. Half a dozen small Mexican children scattered and ran to the house, screaming. I walked to the well, found the bucket half filled with water and dumped it over my head. I turned and headed for the gate. I heard a man shouting something at me in Spanish, but I didn't stop.

The cold water had cleared my head. I swiped at my face with a sleeve.

I was mad clear through. In less than two days, in scarcely more than one, I had fought Shavano, been dragged, and had fought Swope. I was bruised and sore from one end to the other. Every movement was torture.

And why? For no good reason. I had nothing personal against Shavano and certainly did not dislike Swope enough to fight him. I had been drawn into conflict existing in the country long before I came. In some strange way I seemed to be the spark that had set it flaming, and if I wasn't careful I would be consumed by it. Walking, I cursed softly to myself. But I began to hurry, for I wanted to hear what they decided about me if it was not too late.

Approaching the jail, I left the walk and came up under a high barred window to one side of it.

The courthouse, formerly the Spanish governor's headquarters, had adobe walls more than six feet thick. The window was less than two feet square. But I could hear voices because they were raised in intemperate anger.

McGann's voice, deep and thick with rage: "Stand out of the way, Kelso. The sodbusters are going to leave. One way or another, they're going to get off our land or they're going to find themselves under it. We're through playing games with them. We're through trying to scare them. We're in earnest now."

And my father's voice, as deep as McGann's and as angry: "No!"

"Don't interfere, John. If you can't behave like a friend we won't bother to treat you like one. It's your choice."

"Are you threatening me?"

"Warning you." McGann's voice held a pleading note and a note of resentment too. "You owe us something, John."

"Money? Are you using that against me?"

"Don't be thick, sheriff." This was Montour's voice. "We've been using it against you all along and you've been letting us."

"Not for closing my eyes to murder. Maybe I was

81

conscious of those gambling debts. And maybe my sympathies are with cattlemen. But scaring people and killing them are two different things. Even if I'd let you, you couldn't get away with it. They'd get the Army to send some troops in here."

"That's a chance we're going to have to take."

My father's voice rose. "Damn you, I said no!"

McGann's voice was so soft I could scarcely hear. "I was hoping we wouldn't have to do it this way, John."

"What way?"

There was a long silence. Standing beneath the high, small window, I felt cold. What kind of pressure were they going to use on him now?

My father's voice was low and intent. He said, "You'd better explain yourself, McGann. I don't like threats."

"And I don't like to use them. But we have no choice. Our backs are against the wall."

Dunn growled in his harsh and husky voice, "Mart shouldn't have killed Link last night, Kelso."

"That's it, huh? Well, to hell with you. There ain't a jury west of the Mississippi that wouldn't say it was self-defense."

McGann spoke softly, almost regretfully. "There's a jury right here that would say it was deliberate, cold-blooded murder, John. I keep telling you, we don't intend to lose. Too much is at stake. We'll have witnesses, when the time comes, to swear Mart shot Link in cold blood, that Link didn't even have a gun. They'll say Mart's story of all that happened out at Cactus Springs is nothing but a lie to save his skin and that the killing took place here in town. We've spent a lot of time and effort to put you in our debt, John. Now that we don't have to use the debts to keep you in line, I'll tell you something about them. You don't owe them. The poker games were rigged. But this game is too. We've all got plenty of money to see that it stays that way."

McKetridge spoke for the first time. "Damn it, we'd rather have you with us than against us, John. We've been good friends too many years to want it any other way. Why fight a losing game? Throw in with us. We'll burn those damned notes and see to it you get a five-thousand-acre piece of grass to retire to."

"I'll try and forget that bribe you just offered me, Mac. But don't offer me anything again." Father's voice was brittle with anger, as cold as ice.

I could almost see the scene inside the tiny, semi-dark office. Father would be standing behind his desk, unshaven, glowering, more furious than he had ever been in his life. There would be a kind of helplessness apparent in him too, because he knew they could do exactly what they threatened to do. They could bribe witnesses to say what they were supposed to say. They could intimidate Judge Perkins, or bribe him with promises of support in whatever political ambitions he most cherished. They could make him conduct the trial in a manner that would ensure its outcome. It would be cut and dried and Father knew it would. I'd hang for Link's murder and nothing he or anyone else could do would stop it.

What could he do, I wondered. I held my breath, waiting. I realized that I was repeating over and over under my breath, "Tell 'em to go to hell! Tell the bastards to go straight to hell!"

But he didn't tell them that. His voice, when he replied, was shaken and scarcely more than a hoarse whisper. He said, "I've got to have some time. I've got to think about it."

Swope's voice was contemptuous, arrogant. "Sure. Take all the time you want. Take an hour. We'll be over in the Diablo having a beer."

McGann said harshly, "Don't you ever know when to shut up, Swope?"

Swope grumbled something I didn't catch.

McGann said, "One thing more, John. Tell Martin to keep still about the men who were out at Satterlee's last night. If he identifies them . . . well, I won't be responsible for his safety, that's all. Feeling's pretty high over at Fleur de Lis. They liked Link."

I wondered what McGann would say if he knew his own daughter had shot Link, but I knew I'd never be the one to tell him. Nobody would believe it anyway, even if Sue McGann supported the story.

I wanted to go inside. I wanted to give Father my support, to help him with the decision he had to make, but I knew I couldn't. Nobody could help him now. He had to face this wholly by himself, to make a decision and stand by it.

I eased away from the wall and hurried down the street toward home. Helpless anger was smoldering in me. Damn them! It was rotten to lay it on the line the way they had. What father would have a choice under like circumstances? What father would be able to sacrifice his own son on the altar of principle?

I hoped John Kelso would. Perhaps I hadn't yet faced the fact that I would die on the gallows if he did. And maybe it wouldn't have mattered even if I had.

I reached our house and went into the courtyard. I hesitated several moments. Something ominous and threatening seemed to be in the air. A strange feeling of uneasiness possessed me.

Tragedy was building up here in this country I knew so well. It had caught my father and myself on its crest and was sweeping us helplessly along. We could struggle, but we couldn't turn the tide.

10

I crossed the courtyard to the small adobe stable at the far side. I went in, reaching for my bridle hanging beside the door as I did.

Father's horse was in one stall, mine in the other. The combined odors of grain, hay and manure were pleasant and warm and safe. Yet there seemed to be an unpleasant chill about the place I had never noticed before.

I bridled my horse, led him out and flung my saddle onto him. I had no definite plans as to where I was going. Perhaps at that moment I only wanted to get away from town, from the menace that seemed to hang over it. Perhaps I thought that in the solitude of the vast plain I would find the answers my mind was searching for.

I mounted and rode out of the courtyard. I glanced up the street toward the courthouse and saw that the horses of Swope and the Big Four were still racked outside of it. Apparently, then, the discussion had not been finished when I left. Or my father was still trying to talk some sense into them.

I rode through the town, crossed the stream and headed south. The circle I made must have been unconscious, for it surprised me to see The Sentinel ahead.

I grinned ruefully to myself, admitting that I wanted to see Sue and wanted to talk to her. I wanted someone to turn to even though no one could give me the answers I sought. There was simply no way out, no alternative other than the one offered by the Big Four. Father either closed his eyes and officially condoned whatever they chose to do in the days to come or I went on trial and was hanged for murder.

A third alternative presented itself as I rode, one as unpalatable as the first two. I could leave. I could ride away right now, seeing no one, telling no one that I had gone. My disappearance would give Father the freedom of action he had to have. Or would it? Wasn't it possible that with me gone he would slip back to the same state in which he had been when I arrived?

No. I wouldn't run. I didn't want to run. My father

86

meant a great deal to me and so, I had to admit, did Sue. Running would solve nothing. The fight would still have to be fought and Father might still be one of its casualties. It was a cinch the homesteaders would fight back if crowded hard and far enough. There would be many casualties on both sides.

Ahead of me, The Sentinel gradually increased in size as I drew closer to it until I could see the cluster of buildings at its foot.

I remembered the way Sue had been with me last night and excitement touched me. Hell, no, I wasn't going to leave. Neither the Big Four, nor the home-steaders, nor the murder charge hanging over me—none of these things could make me leave. No longer did I want to drift from place to place. My home was here. My future was here. Sue was here too.

I rode into the yard, nodded at a man crossing between bunkhouse and blacksmith shop, and dis-mounted at the back door of the house, which sat on a knoll above the other buildings. I dropped my horse's reins and knocked on the door. Laura McGann answered it.

She was dressed today in a full-skirted cotton dress, very different from the black gown she had worn yes-terday. Her eyes were warm, her full lips parted slightly to show white, even teeth as she smiled at me. "Martin! Come in. Come in this minute!"

I didn't want to go in but I didn't see how I could decently refuse. I asked, "Is Sue here?"

"No. She went riding more than an hour ago. But

that doesn't mean you can't come in, does it? I've some fresh coffee . . ."

I went inside. I suppose I was staring at her but I couldn't help myself. Yesterday, dressed in black, she had seemed older, more experienced, frankly wanton. Today, in the simple, light-colored gingham dress, she seemed like a girl, a helpless, misunderstood, confused young girl.

Her gaze stayed on my face disconcertingly. "Sue ought to be back almost any time. Sit down here in the kitchen and have some coffee. Talk to me for a little while. It gets so lonely here. . . ."

I thought of the things Sue had said about Laura the night before, how she made a pretense of loneliness, how she pursued each new man, how she disappeared sometimes for hours on end. . . . I knew that if all these things were true, Laura was a bitch, taking Mike McGann's love and protection and material things and giving him not even her loyalty in return.

But the picture didn't fit. The innocence of her eyes could not be feigned. No woman could be evil and look as sweet as Laura did.

I felt my face flushing as I accepted a cup of coffee. I had been watching her hips while her back was turned. I had been thinking things no man should think about another's wife.

She was smiling gently at me as though she understood my thoughts. She said softly, "You're lonely too, Martin. I can tell you are."

My voice sounded hoarse. "I've been away—

drifting for a couple of years. Man doesn't make any ties that way."

"Have there been many . . . girls?"

The way she hesitated, there could be no doubt what kind of girls she meant. I felt my forehead grow warm and damp. I mumbled uncomfortably, "A few, I guess."

"Were any of them as pretty as me?"

Suddenly I wanted to get out of there. This conversation was leading in only one direction and while the realization excited me, I knew I was a fool to let it go on this way.

"Were they, Martin?"

"No. Hell, no, they weren't." I blurted that.

She smiled in a strange way and leaned a little closer to me. I picked up my coffee and took a big swallow. It scalded my throat and I began to cough.

When I could control the coughing, I wiped the tears from my eyes with the back of my hand. I felt irritable and angry. If she was laughing at me. . . . But she wasn't. Her eyes were soft and filled with compassion and she was not as close to me as she had been before.

She had withdrawn, but the thoughts her nearness had started churning in my mind had not. She was a peculiar combination—innocence, purity, wanton promise. She could look at me with those beautiful eyes as innocently as a child and all I could think was how much I wanted to go to bed with her. And hate myself because I did.

An older man would have understood the reason for

the seeming incongruity. Laura might look innocent and pure but she was not. Her own thoughts, subtly communicated, were the things that stirred this desire in me.

She changed the trend of the conversation abruptly. She said, "I'll bet you've got an awful temper, Martin. I'll bet after this they don't push you around."

"You mean Link? Last night?"

"Yes. Mike told me about it. I wish I could have seen you!" A strange shine came into her eyes.

"I'm glad you didn't. I was dust and blood from head to foot."

"That wouldn't have bothered me."

My uneasiness returned. I edged back in my chair and shoved it away from the table. I wished Sue would come.

Laura studied me silently for a long time. Her face took on an almost dreamy look. Abruptly she said, "Money isn't everything, Martin."

I looked at her with puzzlement.

"I mean Mike, silly. He's old enough to be my father."

"You knew that when you married him, didn't you?"

"Yes. I suppose I did. Only I thought . . ." She paused and stared at me disconcertingly. "I'm not very old, Martin. There are so many things I don't know." She flushed delicately and lowered her glance. "I didn't know—I mean that when a man gets Mike's age . . . I guess I'm awful, Martin, but I need someone to love me—as much as I want. . . ." She glanced at me and her eyes filled with tears. "A woman isn't supposed to say such things. She isn't supposed to even think them. Now you'll go away thinking I'm nothing but a—" She swallowed as though she couldn't bring herself to say the word.

I sat there uncomfortably, irritated at my own discomfort. But there was sympathy growing in me, sympathy for Laura and for her predicament, admiration for her honesty. . . .

She said softly, "When I think of what it might be like—even in a little bitty line-camp shack—with someone like you . . ."

I said determinedly, "You're Mike's wife. You're Mrs. Mike McGann." I licked my dry lips. "You didn't meet me until yesterday."

"But it seems as though I've known you all my life. We're a lot alike, Martin, whether you realize that or not."

I gulped the rest of my coffee, feeling much as I had so long ago at the bottom of that haystack with Sue. Something was flowing between us, something so strong I could scarcely keep from getting up, going around the table and seizing her in my arms.

Perhaps sensing how near I was to doing it, she withdrew almost imperceptibly from me. Or seemed to. She said, "I suppose I ought to leave him. It would be the only decent thing to do. But where could I go, Martin? What could I do? I don't know anything that would earn a living for me. And I couldn't—I wouldn't want to be like those girls you met while you were away. . . ."

She got up from her chair impatiently. "I'll get you some more coffee." She leaned over to get my cup. Her gown, cut low anyway, dropped slightly as she did and I saw the white swell of her breasts beneath her lacy underwear.

I clenched my hands. Damn it, I'd better get out of here. What was the matter with me, anyhow? I wasn't the kind that went around snorting and pawing after every new woman I met. What the bell was the matter with me today?

I forced myself to think of Sue. Laura poured the coffee cup full, glancing around at me as she did.

Suddenly she gave a little cry. Coffeepot and cup clattered to the floor.

I jumped to my feet. I crossed the room to her. One of her hands was covered with coffee and already turning red. I took hold of her arm and raised her hand to look.

This close, there was a clean fragrance about her. A wisp of her hair touched my face and brushed lightly across it as she turned her head.

Her whole body was shaking, whether from fright, or pain, or something else, I couldn't tell. Because suddenly she was in my arms, warm, strong, but trembling violently.

I forgot the fact that she was burned, as she had so obviously forgotten it. My arms crushed her against me and I lowered my head to kiss her parted lips.

I wondered then and have often wondered since what it is about some women that makes them capable of inspiring such compelling lust in men. I seemed to be drowning, seemed unable to get my breath. It was as though fire instead of blood flowed in my veins. I didn't care that she was Mike McGann's wife, that this was Mike McGann's house. I didn't think about Sue, or my father, or the possible consequences of this act. I ceased to think altogether but I didn't cease to feel. Something burned in me, insistent, demanding, that nothing could ease but the taking of this woman in my arms.

She stopped me herself, struggling, trying to get away. Her voice, filled with shock and terror, stopped me at last before I had gone too far to be stopped at all. "Martin! Oh, Martin, please! Don't—"

It was like coming out of delirium to the world of reality again. I was in Mike McGann's kitchen. I had come here to see Sue. And I was in the act of raping Mike McGann's wife.

I released her so suddenly that she staggered back against the wall and almost fell. I said hoarsely, "I'd better get out of here!"

"Yes, Martin. You had." But she was neither angry nor displeased. Her eyes held something—a promise, perhaps, that another time . . .

I whirled and strode to the door. I flung it open and burst outside. Thank God no one was looking up toward the house as I did. If they had been, they could not have failed to understand what had been going on.

I seized my horse's reins and vaulted to his back. I thundered away, away from the buildings clustered below the knoll upon which the house was built. I headed directly up the slope toward the towering Sentinel behind the house.

My mind was seething, my body sweating but cold as ice. The horse plunged on up the rocky slope. Once I looked back and saw her standing there in the kitchen door, shielding her eyes from the sun with a small, raised hand.

I stopped my horse and stared back at her. I would have given everything I owned or ever hoped to own to have known what expression her face wore just then. Was she devil, or angel, or some frightening combination of both?

Devil? How could a creature as lovely as she be that? It was just—she was more woman than I had ever encountered before. That had to be it. She was lonely, and hungry, and never loved enough by old Mike McGann.

She herself had stopped me, I told myself over and over again. She had stopped me when all she needed to do was keep silent and let me go on.

An angel then. But not that either, else she would not have let me touch her at all.

I spurred my horse on, thundered around the foot of the towering pile of rock and so disappeared from sight of the house and the buildings at its foot.

A woman—but God, what a woman! Her face was like a presence in my thoughts. Remembrance of the warmth, the softness, the delightful shape of her body started my blood to pounding hard again.

I rode at a hard gallop past The Sentinel, down and out across the vast and empty plain. I rode until my horse was lathered and wheezing before I drew him in to a walk.

I dismounted then, removed the saddle and cooled his back by fanning him with the soggy, stinking saddle blanket. I rolled a smoke with hands that shook.

Thank God she was a virtuous woman. Thank God she had stopped me when she had. If she had not . . . I realized that I would do anything she asked of me if fulfillment with her was promised as my reward.

I would kill— I shook my head in self-disgust. No. I would do nothing for her that I would not do anyway. A woman cannot change a man that much.

But however I argued, I wasn't sure. She had instilled in me an overpowering desire for her—desire that she had not permitted to be fulfilled. She had made me want her more than anything else in the world.

Uneasiness touched me. Suppose Sue McGann was right? Suppose Laura was a devil? Suppose she did ask me to get rid of Mike McGann for her?

I felt nausea crawl in my stomach. The thought horrified and sickened me. But what sickened me most was the fact that I didn't know for sure what my answer would be if and when that time ever came.

How many others, I wondered, had she given herself to? If there had been as many as Sue claimed there had . . . And in how many of those others had she planted thoughts of murder?

I had to be wrong. If Sue was right, one of Laura's

men would have tried killing Mike long before this.

I was the one at fault, not Laura, I told myself bitterly. Yet in spite of self-condemnation, in spite of my almost frantic attempts to believe only good of her, a bleak feeling came over me that something had changed, that after today I would never quite be the same again. I was caught up in something. . . .

I tried not to think of Laura, but I couldn't help myself. She filled my thoughts, however hard I tried to turn them to other things.

11

I stayed there in the sun until my horse had cooled. Around me, the grass waved in the light spring breeze. High above, a hawk circled, occasionally swooping low over the grass to seize some careless mouse or young rabbit. After each plummeting raid on the grass, he beat his patient, rising way back to the crags atop The Sentinel where, no doubt, a family of hungry mouths awaited him.

It occurred to me suddenly that Laura had not once mentioned a desire to be rid of Mike McGann. Why, then, was I so sure she would eventually ask me to get rid of him for her? Why, unless the thought was in her mind and through its intensity communicated itself to me? Or was it my own idea?

That thought was frightening, and it was a relief to look up and see Sue McGann galloping toward me half a mile away.

She rode as she almost always rode, in a direct, straight line and as fast as her horse could go. I grinned to myself, watching her. Tension left me and with her coming normality seemed to return to my thoughts.

She returned my grin nervously, swung down from her sweating horse and asked, "How long have you been here?"

"Half an hour, I guess. I came out to see you."

She glanced at my horse, not missing his condition. Sweat and lather had dried on him, leaving his hair stiff and matted. She turned her glance on me questioningly.

I said, "You weren't home."

"No. I wanted to think and I always seem to do that best on a horse." Her eyes studied my horse again, then switched themselves to me. She said, "You must have been riding like the very devil."

I nodded, avoiding her eyes guiltily, angry with myself because I did.

"Did you see Laura?"

I nodded again, glanced up and met her eyes defiantly.

It is possible she misinterpreted my defiance for anger because she was instantly contrite. "I'm sorry, Mart. I have no right to question you. It's just—damn it, I guess I'm jealous. I know her. She'll take you away from me if she can."

I didn't reply. There wasn't much I could say.

Sue's voice was scarcely audible when she spoke again. "Or did I ever really have you?"

I glanced at her guiltily. She was all that Laura was not—youth, honesty, directness. Laura, for all that she conveyed other impressions, was, I admitted reluctantly, both devious and guileful. She was not in love with me or indeed with anyone. But she would use me if she could. I felt suddenly like a rube who has been taken in by a city slicker at the county fair.

I said, "You had me last night and you have me now."

"Do you mean that, Mart?"

I nodded. I did mean it. In this moment of returned sanity I knew it was Sue I wanted and not Laura at all. But how would I feel in Laura's presence? How would I feel when she was near to me, letting me know ever so delicately that she was not unattainable?

Sue said, "All right, Mart. I'll let it go at that." But her voice was lifeless.

I said with sudden anger, "What do you mean, we'll let it go at that? Good God Almighty, I only saw her for a few minutes!"

"But that was long enough, wasn't it? You held her in your arms and if she hadn't protested it'd have gone a damn sight farther than that."

I stared at her in amazement. How could she have guessed so much? How could she have guessed so accurately?

I roared angrily, "You're sure as hell taking a lot for granted!"

"Am I, Mart? Am I really? Then why are you getting so mad?"

"Who's mad?" I spluttered. "Who the hell wouldn't be mad?" But I couldn't go on. It wasn't in me to lie to her, to swear nothing had happened between Laura and myself. I said wearily, "All right. Maybe you guessed right about what happened. But that was all."

Sue winced as though I had struck her. Tears brightened her eyes. She said, "Why, Mart? Oh, why? Didn't I—"

I said angrily, "How the hell should I know why? I'm not the kind that chases everything in skirts. I never had anything like that happen to me before. I don't know why. All I know is, it happened. And I can't even say for sure it won't happen again."

"Are you in love with her?"

"How the hell could I be in love with her? I've only met her twice. I've been with her less than half an hour all told. I don't even know her."

"What did she tell you?"

"Nothing much. She said she wasn't happy with Mike."

"Did she . . . suggest anything?" Sue's face was white.

"No."

"She didn't want you to get rid of Mike?"

"Hell, no!" My answer was almost a shout—too emphatic to be believable. But Sue apparently believed, because she slumped with relief.

I crossed the narrow space separating us and put my hands on her shoulders. She looked up at me with frightened, tearful eyes. "What's going to happen to us, Mart?"

I put my arms around her and held her close. "We'll be all right."

"How can we be?" Her voice was muffled because her face was half hidden against my chest. "Mike and the rest of his friends are going to see to it that you go to trial for killing Link last night. And unless your father gives them a free hand with the homesteaders, they'll see to it you're convicted too. You've got to let me tell Mike that I killed Link." She began to shiver slightly as though she were cold. "It isn't fair for you to take the blame."

I said, "He wouldn't believe you now. Nobody would."

"Let me try anyway."

I shook my head.

She drew away. "I don't need you to protect me."

"I didn't say you did." I stared down at her, wondering why one minute we would be so close and the next ready to jump at each other's throats. "But you sure as hell need somebody."

"If you mean last night—"

"Now who the hell said anything about last night?"

"You were thinking it. You think I'm nothing but a slut that goes out with any man that comes along. You think I'm easy."

"I don't think any such thing."

"You do too."

"Damn it!" I glared at her. "What the hell brought all this on?"

She began to sniffle like a little girl. Her lower lip

trembled. She blubbered, "That damned Laura . . . !"

I put my arms around her again. "To hell with Laura!" I lifted her face and kissed her on the mouth. I put my face against her cheek, which was damp with tears. "Stop talking like a cowhand. You're supposed to be a lady."

"Like Laura, I suppose. Is that what you're thinking?"

"No, damn it, it isn't." I released her and walked angrily to my horse. "Mike still want me out for dinner tonight?"

"How should I know? Why don't you ask him?"

"Not me. I don't want to come anyhow."

I swung to the back of my horse, feeling irritable and unreasonable. Sue glared up at me, but behind the anger in her eyes there was something puzzled, and hurt. I swung my horse and dug spurs into his sides. He jumped with surprise, then pounded away. I didn't even look back.

Women! How the hell was a man supposed to understand them or get along with them? But I was sorry that I'd left Sue this way and only stubbornness kept me from going back. When I finally did look around she and her horse were only a speck, heading toward The Sentinel.

Why had I come out here anyway? I sure as hell hadn't got what I'd expected from Sue.

I let my horse slow to a walk and plod toward home. Anger was stirring in me, not the violent anger I had felt while I was fighting Shavano and Swope, nor the furious outrage I had felt last night at Cactus Springs. This was a different kind—slow and smoldering and lasting.

I hadn't asked for any of the trouble I'd fallen into in the last two days. I hadn't been looking for trouble at all. But I'd found it, or it had found me.

I glanced up when something caught my eye and saw a horseman coming toward me. He was well to the right and would have passed more than a quarter mile away if he had not swung his horse to intercept my own.

It was Mike McGann. He pulled his horse to a halt fifty feet ahead of me and waited.

I pulled in and waited for him to speak, and though I didn't realize it, I was glaring at him.

He said, "Been out at The Sentinel?"

I nodded. "I rode out to see Sue."

"See her?"

"Yes, I saw her. What is this anyhow? Why all the questions?"

"Did you see Laura?"

"Yes, I saw her too."

Something crossed his face, some shadow of doubt or jealousy, and then it went away. He grinned faintly. "What's the matter, did you and Sue have a spat?"

"Yes, we had a spat. What of it?"

His grin widened. "You coming to dinner tonight?"

I stared at him in disbelief. "What is all this to you anyway, some kind of game? Two hours ago you stood in my father's office and threatened to railroad

102

me straight to the gallows. Now you're inviting me to dinner at your house."

"There's nothing personal in any of it, Mart. I like you and always have. Only these goddam sodbusters ain't going to get my land, no matter what I have to do!"

"Even if you have to hang your friends?"

He scowled at me. "Even if I have to do that."

"Then I guess I don't want to be a friend of yours."

His mouth was a thin, hard line. In his eyes I could see some of the steel the man had to possess to have built a thing as enormous and powerful as the McGann Land and Cattle Company. When he spoke, it was in clipped, harsh words. "Get this straight, young fella, and tell your old man to get it straight too. In a month's time they'll be gone—all of them. Maybe some of them will be underground and maybe you and John Kelso will be and maybe I will too. But the sodbusters are going to be gone!"

I said, "You can't exterminate them. They're not coyotes or wolves."

"One of 'em killed your ma. You forgot that?"

I shook my head. "One of them happened to need the doctor the same time she did, that's all. She'd have been the last to blame them for that."

"Your pa blames 'em."

"Not enough to let you exterminate them."

"Don't be too damn sure."

I stared at him. I'd always liked Mike McGann but I didn't like him now. I said, "He won't close his eyes to what you intend to do, even to save my hide. I wouldn't let him even if he would."

"Then you're going to hang." His eyes were cold as a winter wind.

I shrugged. There was no use arguing with him. He hadn't built the McGann Land and Cattle Company by trying to see the other man's side of the argument. And he knew he wouldn't be able to hold it that way.

I moved my horse slightly to one side and he accepted the unspoken invitation to leave, scowling. He rode past me without looking at me again.

I turned my head and watched him ride away. He was a ponderous man atop a horse. He seemed to dwarf the horse with his size.

His hat was crammed down over a leonine mane of graying hair. His neck was as thick, as muscular, as solid as that of one of his bulls.

And his legs . . . Seeming spindly by comparison to his huge torso, they were strong enough to bring a grunt of surprise from his horse if he ever squeezed the animal tightly between them.

He wore a gun but he didn't wear it low the way Jess Swope did. Yet I had seen him draw and fire and hit what he was shooting at so fast that if I blinked my eyes I would miss the entire action.

A formidable opponent in any fight, even by himself, he had twenty punchers working for him who would fight at the drop of a hat.

The homesteaders might be the irresistible force, having, as they did, the full power of the United States government behind them. But McGann and the Big Four . . . They were the immovable object.

Uneasiness possessed me as I turned and rode toward town. For the first time I faced a fact—that if Father did not give in I would hang for the murder of Link.

No longer was it merely a threat to be lightly brushed aside. McGann and the others were in deadly earnest. They were fighting for their lives, for the land and the way of life they had spent their lives and shed their blood to build.

In another week—in another day perhaps—the nights would be filled with the terrifying sounds of many hoofs galloping across the grass. The sky would be lighted with the orange glare of leaping flames. There would be shouts of pain, and screams from the dying, and whimpering from the hurt and bereaved. If father wanted to win this one he had better send off a wire for the Cavalry right away.

Frowning and worried, I lifted my horse to a jogging trot and continued on toward town.

12

While I was still half a mile from the town, I could tell that something was wrong. There was sound in the air, drifting toward me from it, sound that came and went like distant thunder on the horizon. Only this sound more closely resembled the droning around a hive of bees.

It was the sound of voices, of many voices, and that could mean only one thing. The homesteaders, realizing that they had to fight or die, were organizing for the fight.

I entered the town from its northern side, the way I had entered it two days ago when I first came home, but it was a different town than it had been then. There was nothing sleepy about it now. The Mexican families had retired in terror to their homes and the streets were filled with angry homesteaders.

Their wagons choked the square. Cooking fires sent up thin plumes of smoke from beside the wagons. Women clustered in small groups, talking with worried looks on their drawn faces. Even the children's play was subdued.

Away from the square, on the streets of the town, the men moved about, also gathering into groups. Their talk, however, was angry and often punctuated by shouts. Many of them carried new guns, probably purchased only today. Others carried ancient shotguns, or smooth-bore rifles. In one man's belt I saw an old flintlock pistol.

Those who had no firearms carried axes or pitchforks. I wondered inwardly how they would fare against a hundred mounted, armed, toughened cowhands who had lived with violence of one kind or another every day of their lives. It would be slaughter, I realized. The cowhands would cut through them like a scythe through grain, leaving them broken and scattered behind.

While yet half a block from the courthouse, I was forced to halt my horse by a mob of homesteaders clogging the street. Beyond them someone was shouting at them. I stared at him and saw that it was Shavano.

"Are we going to wait," he howled hoarsely, "until they've picked us off one by one? They'd have killed Satterlee last night if the sheriff's kid hadn't interfered. Maybe they've killed him anyhow. Last I heard he wasn't no more'n holdin' his own. You, Johanson! You might be next on their murder list. Or you, Shulman. You might be the one. Any of us could be. I say we'd better get together right now before it's too late to do anything!"

"What can we do that won't just make it worse?"

Shavano fixed his glance on the man who had spoken. He roared, "You know your Bible, Hays. An eye for an eye and a tooth for a tooth. Every time they do something to one of us, we do it to them in return. Right now I'd say it was time we roped one of them and dragged him up the street until he's damn near dead!"

The crowd roared approval. I pushed my horse into them and started through. Father ought to know about this before they carried out their threat. Because if they did . . .

Angry faces turned toward me, a dangerous explosiveness in them all. I touched spurs to my horse's sides and forced him through. He reared once, narrowly missing a homesteader with his pawing front hoofs as he dropped to the ground again.

I heard the word "cowman" uttered by several of them as though it were a curse. Hands pulled at my legs, trying to drag me from my horse.

A dangerous mob. A mob that might do anything. Several voices rose. "Here's one of the bastards now. Let's drag this one."

I dug spurs deep this time and the horse lunged ahead, bowling them over to right and left. A pitchfork jabbed him in the flank and he began to buck. Caught by surprise and off balance anyway, I sailed out of the saddle on the second jump.

I struck a man as I went down, breaking the force of my fall. I fought to my feet and began swinging furiously. I smashed a fist into one man's nose and saw it burst. But they were too many and they came from the front, from both sides and from the rear. I went down with half a dozen of them on top of me.

Shavano's bellowing voice stopped them and pulled them away from me. I got up and I'm sure my face was white with fury. Shavano dusted me off solicitously with one hand while he yelled, "Boys, you got the wrong man. This here's the sheriff's kid, the one that saved Satterlee from gettin' dragged to death last night. This one here is with us, by God!"

He had a rank, sour smell. His long underwear, which he wore in lieu of a shirt, was yellow with sweat and dirt. He looked as though he had neither shaved nor washed for a week, and he probably hadn't because he still smelled of pigs. More than anything else I wanted to smash his mouth with my fist but I knew that if I did I was finished. I'd never get clear of this mob without him.

It rankled to be saved by someone I despised as I did Shavano. He was the worst of the homesteader bunch for all that he was their leader. He was in this for money and nothing else. He was blackmailing McGann for twenty thousand dollars by holding Comanche Springs. If McGann would dig up the money and pay him off . . .

That might be the solution, I thought. Without Shavano, the homesteaders might lose heart, pack up and leave. Maybe it wouldn't be fair but at least they'd stay alive.

Shavano had stopped dusting me off and was now facing the crowd. He yelled, "Maybe we can get us more than one to drag behind a horse. Kelso here was out at Cactus Springs last night. He knows who the men were that dragged Satterlee."

The voices of the homesteaders were like echoes of Shavano's voice. "Who were they, Kelso? Give us their names. Tell us where to find them!"

I thought to myself sourly, "Try the Diablo Saloon," but I didn't say anything. I edged to my horse and picked up his reins. I started to lead him through the mob.

I hoped my face didn't show them the stubborn refusal I felt. I hoped I could get in the clear before I was forced to either give them the names or flatly refuse.

Maybe I'd give those names to my father, if and when he decided he wanted them. So the men responsible could be arrested and prosecuted according to the law. But I wasn't going to give them to a mob any more than I was going to let the Big Four intimidate me into forgetting them.

Shavano pushed up beside me. I felt stifled and surrounded and a little desperate because I knew I'd be lucky if I got through this mob alive. He said in a hoarse whisper, "The names, man. The names! If you don't give them those names you're in trouble. Don't you realize that?"

I said, "Sure I realize it. But you can go to hell, Shavano. The man's dead because they dragged Satterlee. Let it go at that. If you push it you and every man here is going to be sorry."

"Threatening us?"

"Me? What have I got to threaten with? I'm just telling you, or trying to tell you, what you're up against. The Big Four can raise a hundred mounted men to fight you, every one of them able to shoot better than the best damn man you've got. They killed Comanches by the hundreds when they took this land. They'll kill homesteaders by the hundreds to keep it. So think twice before you spit in their faces."

I could see the edge of the crowd ahead. It couldn't have been more than forty feet, but it seemed like a hundred miles. They were bunching ahead of me now, and I was making practically no progress.

I stared over their heads, stared at the sheriff's office

half a block away. Even if father had been standing in the doorway it was doubtful if he'd have been able to pick me out, hidden as I was by the crowd.

I was scared suddenly, scared clear through for the first time since I'd come home. Up in Colorado I'd seen a man hanged by a mob and it had been an ugly thing I knew I could never forget. Now the same thing was about to happen to me. The only thing that could save me was the names of those out at Cactus Springs last night.

I pushed against the crowd blindly, leaving angrily muttering men behind. I seemed to be in a kind of trance as my mind battled it out.

Why shouldn't I tell? I thought. Why shouldn't men who inflict violence on others be the ones to pay for it? Why should I die to protect them?

And yet it wasn't a question of that at all, I realized. This was a matter of personal pride, a question of whether or not I was going to let them intimidate me. I was not connected with the sheriff's office, officially at least, and yet everything I did would reflect upon it.

Thirty feet still remained. And they were closing in more solidly.

Shavano whispered hoarsely, "Tell them, man! Tell them! You've waited too long already!"

I drew my revolver and jammed it roughly into his side. The sound of the hammer cocking was loud and clear in the momentary silence that followed his words.

I raised my head and shouted, "Open up a path. I've got a gun in Shavano's guts and I'll blow them out if a one of you puts a hand on me. God damn it, open up a path!"

I was completely halted now, unable to move in any direction. My horse was growing restive and scared with so many men pressing against him from all sides. He kept crowding up against me, nudging me, but there was no place I could go to get out of his way.

If I was jostled severely, I might accidentally pull the trigger of my gun. And if that happened nothing on earth could save my neck.

Impasse. I wondered if they held Shavano in enough esteem to care whether they saved his life or not. I whispered, "Talk to them, damn you! I meant exactly what I said. I'll blow your guts out if anything goes wrong!"

He turned his head and stared at me. He was sweating and his face was shiny. He put up a hand and wiped the sweat off his forehead with the back of it.

Obviously he decided I would do as I said I would. For he raised his voice and yelled, "Do what he says! Open up and let us through. Don't try anything stupid. He can kill me before you can get him away from me!"

The faces of those nearest me were murderous. A moment ago I had been one of them, accepted because Shavano told them I had interfered last night in Satterlee's behalf. Now I was solidly on the other side again and their expressions told me what they would like to do to me.

To hell with them. I wasn't on their side and didn't want to be. Neither was I on the side of the cowmen who were trying to drive them out. All I wanted was to stay neutral and by God, I was going to stay that way.

Slowly they began to edge sullenly aside and the narrowest of paths began to open up.

Neutral, I thought bitterly. That meant, in this case at least, being hated bitterly by both sides. Those punchers out at Cactus Springs had hated me enough last night to drag me to death behind a horse. This bunch hated me enough to string me up right now. Yet somehow, out of all this blind hatred, Father was going to have to bring order and peace.

The edge of the mob was now less than fifteen feet away. And the way was clear—except for one hothead no more than eighteen years old who stood squarely in my path, a double-barreled shotgun in his hands.

Shavano howled, "Get out of the way, Russ! Put that damned shotgun down! You'll kill me along with him!"

There was no relaxing in the young man's almost fanatical expression. His eyes burned. His mouth was set in a bloodless, thin straight line. His jaws were clenched so hard the muscles bunched. I glanced at his knees and saw they were trembling.

I was not as close to safety as I had thought. The young man might do anything, and I'd never know what it was until he did it.

He was five or six feet ahead of me now. The bore

of the double-barrel was pointing straight at my mid-section.

My belly began to twitch. I knew if I didn't do something immediately it was going to be too late.

Shoving Shavano violently away from me, I kicked violently at the same time. I felt my foot strike the barrel of the shotgun and almost immediately heard the blast of it.

Powder stung my face and I felt its heat. But the shot whistled over my head, roaring like a high gust of wind.

I was moving now, continuously and as swiftly as I could. Whirling, I vaulted to my horse's back and sank my spurs in him.

He struck the young man with the shotgun squarely, knocking him aside and down. He thundered along the path that had previously opened up and into the clear. I leaned low over his withers and raked him with the spurs.

Shots racketed behind me, pistols, rifles, shotguns, recognizable by their deep and heavy sounds. Bird-shot pelted my back and my horse's rump. He seemed to squat and then to run faster than he had been running before.

I tried to haul him in before Father's office but he plunged on past. I whirled him by force and he nearly fell. I swung down and plunged across the gallery and into my father's office, colliding violently with him as he came to the door. The horse hesitated for a fraction of an instant, then ran down the street trailing the reins.

Father slammed the office door and turned to face me with his back to it. "What the hell was that all about?"

"I tried to get through 'em is all." I was panting and out of breath and now my knees were beginning to shake. I sat down abruptly. "They stopped me. First they were going to drag me behind a horse to get even for Satterlee. Then when Shavano told 'em who I was, I was a hero until I refused to name the other men out at Cactus Springs last night. Then they wanted to hang me."

Father's face was pale but it was angry too. "I thought it was just talk out there—until the shooting started. They've been hollerin' all morning—ever since you left."

He stared at me steadily and disconcertingly for several moments. "How'd you get out of it?"

"I jammed a gun into Shavano's ribs. I told 'em I'd kill him if they didn't let me through."

He nodded, studied me for a moment more in a way I felt was approving, even if grudgingly so. He turned and stared out the window into the street and his expression drew me instantly to the window at his side.

I wanted to ask him if he'd decided anything but there wasn't time right now. The homesteaders, led by Shavano, were heading in an angry mob directly toward the jail.

13

There is something frightening about men gathered together into a mob. Individual conscience disappears. The men composing it cease to be individuals capable of independent thought and action. They become but a part of the group, conscienceless, merciless, caught up in some kind of hysteria they cannot control. All the leader has to do is shout a suggestion and no matter how wild, how unthinkable that suggestion may be, it is taken up immediately by the howling members of the mob.

They almost always regret their actions later and are remorseful over what they have done. But it is too late then—too late for the unfortunates hanging by their necks, or beaten to death, or maimed for life.

It was like watching some kind of monster stir and come to life. They came toward us slowly, with Shavano leading them. Their faces were ugly with anger because I had escaped. They were determined too. They had taken the initial step toward violence by threatening me and shooting at me when I escaped. Now that the initial step had been taken, they would go on, more easily, to the next violent step.

Father said softly, "I wouldn't mind seeing the Big Four and about a hundred men ride into town right now."

I glanced across the square toward the Diablo Saloon. Perhaps a dozen cowhands were clustered on the walk in front of it. Even as I watched they untied their horses, mounted and thundered away toward the edge of town. Help was too far away to do us any good. I said, "You've always handled whatever came along before. Getting old or something?"

His neck darkened. He glanced at me and there was anger in his eyes. "Don't get smart with me."

I grinned, and suddenly we seemed close—closer than we had been in years. When he looked back out of the window there was less of doubt in the set of his mouth, more of confidence.

Shavano shuffled across toward the couthouse, looking like an old, yellowed and very dirty bear. The others kept almost abreast of him. He halted a dozen yards from the door and yelled, "Sheriff!"

I glanced aside at my father's face. I could see the anger mounting in him. Shavano's tone had been curt, arrogant, as though he held the upper hand and meant to exploit it for all it was worth.

Father whirled, went to the door and yanked it open. He stood there silently in the doorway, glaring at Shavano. Shavano's eyes shifted. His tone was blustering. "We want the names of the men out at Cactus Springs last night. We want 'em now. You get them out of that kid of yours and do it quick!"

Father said, "Shavano, you push me a little more and I'll throw you in jail. I'll keep you there until you rot."

"We want those names. You got five minutes to get 'em out of him."

"And you've got five minutes to clear the street. Starting now." He pulled his watch out of his pocket and glanced at it.

A grumbling began in the crowd, a grumbling that grew in volume as the seconds passed. I wondered if Father had gambled too much, if he had overplayed his hand. Supposing they did not disperse within the five minutes he had given them? What would he do? If he opened fire on them. . . . But that was unthinkable. He wouldn't do that.

He said, "A minute's gone."

Shavano yelled, "The names. We want 'em, sheriff, and we're going to get 'em!"

Father looked at his watch again. He waited a moment and then said calmly. "Two minutes gone."

But I was not his son for nothing, and I could see, even if the others could not, a kind of desperation in his face. He had, in his mind, already gone to the five-minute deadline and he didn't know what he was going to do.

The seconds ticked away endlessly. The mob behind Shavano showed no sign of withdrawal or even hesitation.

Father said, "Three."

A man in the crowd yelled, "We'll telegraph for the Army."

Father said, "They won't come. Not unless they're called in by the recognized authorities of the town or territory."

"Then we'll appeal to the Governor."

Father shrugged. "That's up to you."

The crowd out there was growing. Men came from the rear and sides of it, some out of curiosity but some because they knew what was going on and wanted to be a part of it.

I glanced beyond them at the square where the homesteaders' wagons and fires were. Women and children were huddled there in a group, their faces white, staring at the scene in the street with silent terror.

Father said, "Four minutes gone. Now I'll tell you what I'm going to do when it reaches five. I'm coming out there and I'm going to arrest Shavano. If there's one sign of resistance I'm going to kill him."

He took a couple of steps to the middle of the puncheon walk. He seemed sure now, almost cold. He had decided upon a course of action and would go through with it without qualm or hesitation.

A dangerous course of action, because there was sure to be resistance from someone in that crowd. They wouldn't let him have Shavano. They'd resist, and he'd kill Shavano, and after that nothing on earth could save him from their wrath. He'd be riddled before he could retreat or turn his gun on them.

I crossed the office running and seized a double-barreled shotgun from the rack. I snatched a handful of ten-gauge shells loaded with buck. I broke the action of the gun as I crossed to the door, and punched two in. Then I shoved the rest into the right-hand pocket of my pants.

I stepped out of the door with the gun pointed negligently at the mob. At this range—with two ten-gauge barrels loaded with buck—I would kill from three to a dozen men with the initial blast.

Father could hardly have known that I was there. He expected no help from me and probably didn't even want it. He was a giant again—he was John Kelso—he was a living legend with the fastest gun in this part of New Mexico.

He wouldn't ask for help but he needed it. I stepped out to the edge of the gallery into the sun so that none of them could fail to know that I was there.

That last minute was the longest of my life, before or since. It ticked away endlessly. Father stood out there in the street, his head bare, his ponderous gold watch in his left hand, his eyes upon it as though there were no mob, no explosive situation that he would meet when a minute had ticked slowly past.

And yet in spite of my dread, in spite of my horror of what was happening, of what was going to happen, in spite of my own certainty that it would end with both of us riddled and dead in the dust, there was a gloriousness about that moment rarely equaled in man's experience. I felt a strong pride in my father because he had come back, because he was again the man he had always been before my mother died. If he died he would die proudly and honorably, doing his duty as he saw it. And no man could ask for more than that when the moment of dying comes.

The last minute must be nearly gone, I thought.

Father lifted his head and stared hard at Shavano. He said, "Ten seconds, you. Make up your Goddamned mind."

My breath sighed out slowly. I felt weak, drained of strength, and little spots swam before my eyes. I realized I had been holding my breath.

Shavano began to wilt. His eyes shifted from my father's and stared at the ground at his feet. He shifted his weight from one foot to the other. Without speaking, he turned and shoved his way through the crowd. He had seen sure death in my father's eyes and it must have turned his insides to ice.

It was the beginning of the end. Shavano's retreat left the mob without a leader and it began to crumble as soon as Shavano turned his back on my father's chilling eyes.

Across the street in the square, half a dozen women began to weep hysterically with relief.

Father stood there like a rock, glaring at every member of the crowd that would look at him, and waited while they dispersed and shuffled away.

I backed across the gallery and into the door. I broke the shotgun and ejected the two shells. I dropped them, along with those in my pocket, into the desk drawer. Then I replaced the shotgun on the rack.

I returned to my place at the window just as Father stepped inside the door. His face was sweating heavily but otherwise there was no sign of strain in him.

I said, "They'll wire the Governor. They'll ask for troops. How long will it take?"

"A week if everything goes all right. It could take more."

"Will the troops be sent?"

He nodded.

"And that means the end of the Big Four."

He nodded again. "Unless they clean the whole thing up in the next week or ten days."

I said, "Even then they'll lose. With troops in here the homesteaders will all come back."

"Those that can."

I was silent for a long time after that, staring out the window at the square across the street. The whole thing was wrong, I thought. Everybody but the government recognized the cowmen's right to their land, recognized the right of possession as valid. Now the government was offering it to anyone who came along. It was little wonder the cowmen were incensed. And used to meeting threats themselves, they were meeting this one themselves.

Father said, "I wish you'd pull out—for a while at least."

"Jump bail?"

He snorted. "That's a ridiculous charge and you know damn good and well it is. If you killed Link at all, it was self-defense."

"What do you mean, if I killed him?"

He stared hard at me and I had difficulty meeting his eyes. He said, "If Link was draggin' you, how the hell did you get loose?"

My mind searched frantically for a believable

122

answer to that. It found none, and so I said, "How the hell should I know? I did, that's all. Have you ever been dragged? Did you remember everything that happened?"

"What was Sue McGann doing all this time?"

I said sourly, "I wasn't watching her. My eyes were full of dust."

"Then how the hell could you see to shoot?"

I said, changing the subject, "Why do you want me to leave?"

"That's kind of a stupid question, isn't it? Even for you?"

I nodded.

He said, "If you weren't here, I'd have a free hand without worrying about you going to trial for killing Link."

I said, "And if I left, I'd still be the sheriff's kid, getting out of the way as usual. I'd come back when it was nice and safe for me and I'd still be John Kelso's kid. Maybe I want to be Martin Kelso for a change. Maybe that's why I want to stay."

He glanced at the gun rack across the room. "You were Martin Kelso a few minutes ago when you came outside carrying that ten-gauge."

"How did you know?"

"I looked around as you were going in."

I said, "I didn't scare anybody. You made Shavano fold."

He grunted. "I still wish you'd leave. McGann and the others mean what they say. They can railroad you if they make up their minds to it."

I shrugged. "Maybe they can, but they'll have to do more than threaten to." I could feel myself getting stubborn about it. Maybe I wasn't very smart, but I wasn't going to run away.

Apparently he realized that I meant exactly what I said, because he didn't mention leaving again. He said, "Then we'd better round up the Big Four and talk to them. It's time they listened to some sense."

I didn't know what he meant by that and I didn't ask. At least he was through sitting in his chair with a bottle at his side. At least he was going to act.

14

There were signs of activity across the street in the square as we stepped out the door. And there was a changed atmosphere about the town.

Already two or three of the wagons were pulling out of the square, heading either to the camp ground down in the cottonwoods or back out to their occupants' homestead claims.

Sullenness was visible in the faces of all the homesteaders we saw and those that looked at us had open hatred in their eyes. But the violence was gone from them. Once again they were a peaceful people, for all their resentment and their fear.

Not that they would stay that way, I thought. Shavano might be able to arouse them again or another leader might emerge. Or some new outrage like the one last night might bring another near rebellion on.

In the meantime, I could be sure a wire had gone to the territorial governor and with it a request for troops. I didn't know the man but if he was as politically minded as Judge Perkins was he wouldn't be able to ignore it, if indeed he wanted to. He'd have to forward the request to the nearest Army post.

A week, I thought. A week to solve the unsolvable. One thing was sure. If a solution was to be found, both sides were going to have to give partway. Neither could maintain the firm whole-hog-or-none stand they had been taking thus far.

We walked down the street toward home and for the first time since releasing him, I wondered about my horse. I supposed he had gone home. We would probably find him standing in front of the stable waiting to be let in.

I was not disappointed. He was standing where I had expected him to be and as we entered the courtyard he turned his head to look at us.

Father went into the stable to saddle his horse and I took the saddle off mine and rubbed him down while I was waiting. Then we both rode out, with Father in the lead.

Dunn's Square D was the only one of the Big Four ranches south of town, so we rode out north. And since Mike McGann was the unspoken leader of the four, we headed toward The Sentinel.

My horse, being tired, wanted to follow along behind, but I forced him up abreast of Father's horse.

I asked, "Do you really think they'll listen to you? Any better than they have before?"

He didn't reply or even look at me. The fact that he didn't gave me my answer as eloquently as any words.

The sun was high in the sky now, and growing hot. The horizon held the towering shapes of windmills, the uneven rows of fences and the dark-red shapes of grazing cattle. The sky was blue, dotted with scattered, puffy, high clouds. When we drew abreast of Montour's Fleur de Lis, something else appeared on the horizon—a dust cloud rising from the hoofs of many horses paralleling our course and heading for The Sentinel. They were traveling faster than we and the dust cloud drew ahead rapidly.

Later, when we drew abreast of McKetridge's Anchor, I watched the horizon for a similar dust cloud. I failed to see it and so assumed their riders had already reached The Sentinel.

We'd find them all there, planning their strategy, planning whatever violence they had in mind. And if that hardened bunch of riders ever left The Sentinel . . .

It seemed to take forever to reach the place though I know it took only a little longer than usual and this because my horse was tired. The towering rock shape of The Sentinel grew in size and so did the buildings clustered at its foot. While we were still a mile away I saw the horses in the yard below the house. There must have been nearly a hundred of them and just by milling around they raised a cloud of dust that towered as high as the monstrous house sitting on its knoll.

126

Father didn't increase his pace though I knew he must have seen them too. I glanced at his face and studied it.

It was as hard, as immovable as the rock face of The Sentinel standing behind McGann's house. His eyes were narrowed against the dust and glare. His jaw seemed to have been hacked out of granite. His mouth was a thin, straight line.

Two days had certainly worked a change in him, I thought. Perhaps something like this had been what he needed. Perhaps, having been a man of violence all his life, he had needed violence to help him recover from the shock of Mother's death.

I wished that I could have seen him doing some of the things he had done during the course of his life. But he had never let me go along with him before.

I had watched him this morning though. And I could watch him today when he confronted the Big Four and their assembled crews.

We rode into the yard, through it and directly on up the side of the knoll to the rear of the house. I saw Dunn's men in the yard, squatted in the shade of the north side of the barn, and Montour's, and McKetridge's and McGann's. I saw a few independent ranchers too and a few men I couldn't place because I didn't know them from before I'd gone away.

They were silent, or talking softly among themselves like men do before going into battle. A few of the younger ones looked a little scared and seemed to be trying to hide their fear with a show of bravado. I saw one of Montour's men who had been at Cactus Springs last night looking at me with open hatred in his eyes. A friend of Link's, I supposed. He couldn't blame Sue for his friend's death so he had fastened the blame on me.

Father dismounted deliberately near McGann's back door. It was closed but we could hear voices through it. Father dropped his reins and I followed suit. We walked to the door and Father knocked imperatively.

McGann answered it. There was surprise in his eyes as he said, "I thought you were in trouble back in town. Some of the boys—"

Father said, "It's over now. They've gone back home."

McGann switched his glance to me. "Heard you damn near got mobbed when you got back to town."

I said, "It came out all right."

McGann looked from me to Father and back again as though he saw some similarity and was weighing it. He said belatedly, "Well, hell, come on in. Don't stand out there in the sun."

Father went in and I followed. The other members of the Big Four were there along with Swope, Laura McGann and some of the Big Four foremen. The kitchen, for all its size, seemed crowded. There was a bottle of whiskey on the table, the cork lying beside it. There were some empty glasses, and some partly filled, and several coffee cups. Laura tried to catch my eye but I deliberately avoided looking at her.

McGann closed the door, turned and said, "Nice to

128

have you out, John, but what's the occasion?"

"Don't play dumb with me. I saw that bunch leave the Diablo a while ago. I knew they'd come running home and I knew exactly what you'd do. I came to tell you to forget it."

"Oh. You mean those men down in the yard?"

Father grunted something contemptuously. "Jesus, you're innocent, ain't you. What you figuring to do first?"

"Well, since you seem to have it figured out, we're going to run that bunch of homesteaders out of town to start it off."

"Just like that, huh?"

"Just like that. There ain't an ounce of guts in the whole kit and caboodle of 'em."

"Sure of that, huh? The only man with any guts is one with rope burns on his hands?"

"Well . . ."

"Plenty of those homesteaders were in the war, Mike. A pitchfork ain't the only thing they know how to use."

Swope broke in, "Don't listen to him. Let's go clean 'em out."

Father stared icily at Swope, then back at McGann. "I think you only intend to hooraw 'em, Mike. But what about Swope? You think he won't be shooting to kill? And how about some of the others in that bunch out there?"

Mike scowled. I kept still. I knew they'd resent anything I said because of my age. Father said, "By now they've telegraphed the Governor for troops. The troops will arrive in less than a week. When they do get here, do you think for a minute every man jack of you isn't going to be held responsible for what he's done? Judge Perkins' court is going to be the busiest place in the county—next to the public scaffold I'll have to put up in the square."

McGann barked, "What do you want? What the hell's your idea?"

Father said, "A deal. I can put my own pressure on the Governor if I've got anything to bargain with. He doesn't want troops in here. He doesn't want anything that even looks like an insurrection while he's in office."

Montour asked, "What are you getting at?"

"I want the men that dragged Satterlee and fired his barn. I want them in jail and I want them to go to trial."

There was an immediate hubbub in the room, with every one of the cowmen present protesting at once. Father waited until it was relatively quiet again and then he said, "It's the only thing that will stop those troops. I've got to be able to go to the Governor and show him that the law is being upheld."

Swope shouted, "It's a trick, a stinking goddam trick! If he puts them in the clink it throws out your whole case against Mart for killin' Link. He's just tryin' to get out from under. We got him where it hurts and he's squirmin' to get loose!"

Again there was confusion in the room. Most of the men appeared to agree with Swope.

130

Father shrugged. He looked mild for the first time today and I knew him well enough to realize that he was much more angry than he had been before.

My own inclination was to be disgusted with the deal he had offered them. It didn't agree with my picture of a good lawman—one who made deals before he dared arrest lawbreakers. But I could understand the pressure that forced him to do it. A hundred armed men itching for a fight are not to be taken lightly.

McGann stared at the others, in turn. He stared back at Father again. He said, "I'm not the big noise here. We'll have to talk it over. Will you wait outside a few minutes?"

Father nodded and crossed to the door. He stepped outside and I followed. I reached for tobacco nervously, made a smoke, then handed the sack to him. We lighted up and walked over to the shade of a cottonwood, where we hunkered down against the trunk.

I asked, "Think they'll go for it?"

He nodded calmly. "They've got no choice. Oh, maybe not right away. They'll ride to town and show the homesteaders they haven't been bluffed out. But the men will all be under orders not to use their guns. And when they've done that, they'll agree to hand over the men that were at Satterlee's."

He had hardly finished speaking when the door opened and McGann came out. He crossed to us and said, "I don't know, John. You'll have to let them think it over for a while."

"Meantime, you're coming in to town?"

McGann nodded, staring at Father with penetrating eyes.

Father got up. "I'll go on ahead. Just remember, Mike. I'll hold every damned one of them individually accountable for what he does."

McGann nodded. We got our horses, mounted up and left the yard. We rode down off the knoll, through the assembled men and out in the direction of town.

Once clear of the ranch, Father lifted his horse to a lope and I followed suit. My horse was tired but it was important that we reach town ahead of the Big Four and their men.

We had gone several miles before I glanced back and saw the cloud of dust rise between us and The Sentinel. Father saw it too and spurred his horse.

One little incident in town would be all that it would take. One small outburst of violence and then it would be beyond the ability of any man or group of men to control.

He wanted to be in town to make sure that one little incident did not occur. I felt as though we were both sitting in the same room with a box of dynamite, waiting for it to explode.

I glanced aside at his face. He didn't seem like the same man he had been two days ago. Yet I didn't like the deal he had offered McGann. Somehow or other law by compromise seemed indecent to me.

And yet, I reasoned, wasn't it better to have the law emerge triumphant, by whatever means, than to break down and fail altogether?

I scowled as I rode. I should leave questions like that to men with more brains and education than I possessed.

My horse was nearly beat when we reached the town but we did reach it and half a mile ahead of the cowmen at that. I took the horses home as soon as Father had dismounted at his office door.

I didn't bother to rub them down, just unsaddled, threw down some hay and closed the stable door. Then I hurried to the street.

I was in time to see the cowmen enter town and I stood at the entrance of our little courtyard watching them.

There was something awesome, something very impressive in it, and I was struck by the notion that they were a vanishing race just as the Indians had been fifty years before.

They filled the street, from side to side. McGann, Montour, McKetridge, Dunn and Swope rode abreast at their head. Behind the five came the respective foremen, and behind them the smaller independent ranchers from the boundaries of the Big Four ranches.

Dusty, hardened, sun-blackened men, they were as competent-looking a fighting force as I had ever seen. Rifles lay across their knees. Revolvers sagged in holsters at their sides.

The few homesteaders left in town drew back into doorways, trying to make themselves inconspicuous. And Father stood spread-legged before his office door as though daring the cowmen to start something.

15

There was something truly magnificent about the sight as the cowmen rode their horses across the square, for as they passed Father standing before the low adobe courthouse, they spurred and yelled almost as one man.

They thundered past, enveloping him in their dust, crossed the square where so recently the homesteaders' wagons had been and where some of their fires still smoldered, and pulled their plunging mounts to a halt in front of the Diablo Saloon.

I watched until their hundred horses were racked and tied, until the hundred had trooped into the Diablo and disappeared from sight. Then I walked through the pall of dust still hanging in the street to where my father stood.

He grinned sparely and said, "They made their point, didn't they?"

"They did. Now what?"

He shrugged. "They'll whoop it up for two or three hours and then go home. I don't think there will be too many homesteaders staying around in town tonight."

He turned and went into his office. He said, "Go get yourself some supper, Mart. Bring mine back when you come. I ought to stay here."

I nodded, turned away from him and headed down the street toward home. Now that I had time, I rubbed both horses down, grained and watered them and returned them to their stalls. By the time I had finished and washed, supper was ready inside the house.

Francisca's expression was sober and worried, but she didn't speak. She served my supper silently and prepared a tray for me to take Father when I had finished eating.

Carrying the tray, I left the house and walked down to the courthouse. I took the tray inside, watched as Father began to eat, then went back outside again.

The sun was setting in the west, laying its salmon-colored glow upon the town and the land beyond. Clouds flamed in the sky. Across in the square perhaps a dozen small, dirty Mexican children were searching for things the homesteaders might have left behind.

From the Diablo came the sound of a piano, the more penetrating sounds of a woman's voice singing in Spanish. Almost obscuring those sounds were the boisterous voices of the cowmen inside.

Peaceful. Ordinary. And yet there was a feeling about the town—of waiting, of apprehension. Or perhaps it was just apprehension inside myself. This was not a peaceful town and could not be until the burning issue of the homesteaders had been settled.

I stared gloomily at the Diablo across the square. The doors opened and a man came out.

At this distance I could not recognize him. Light was fading rapidly from the clouds. But as he moved away after looking to right and left along the street, I knew him at once by the peculiar, springy way he walked. It was Jess Swope.

There was reason now for the apprehension I had felt. Swope wouldn't leave the revelry inside the Diablo unless he had a good reason for doing so. Fiery talk, the kind being indulged in by the cowmen tonight, was Jess Swope's meat.

His horse was racked several doors from the Diablo. He walked to the animal, untied him and swung to his back.

At a walk, he crossed a corner of the square and headed south. And I discovered that I was hurrying in the same direction. Swope had to be up to something, leaving the Diablo this way.

I glanced once at my father's office but I knew there wasn't time to tell him what I suspected. There was only time to follow Swope and try to keep him in sight.

Fortunately Swope never lifted his horse to a gait faster than a walk, or I would have lost him in the dusk. As it was, I managed to stay less than a block behind him all the way through Rio de Oro's twisting back streets.

A thought kept occurring to me, one I'd had earlier today. Shavano was the key to this whole business. He was the homesteaders' self-appointed leader but he was also accepted by them all. I had thought it might pay the Big Four to buy him off. Now I was willing to bet that Swope had thought of a cheaper way, because he was headed straight for the homesteader encampment along the creek.

He rode steadily and purposefully but unhurriedly.

The thought struck me that he was like an executioner, savoring the business that lay ahead. One thing was certain. He was taking his life in his hands going down there all alone. Doing so took either the courage to face them all to achieve his end, or contempt for the whole outfit, a belief that they hadn't the guts to attack him no matter what he did.

He seemed to know exactly where he was going, and as the dusk grew deeper, as we penetrated deeper into the grove of cottonwoods where the home-steaders' wagons were, I realized that he had to know where he was going. That probably explained his lack of fear. He was either going to meet someone or heading toward a wagon separated from the main homesteader encampment, at its very edge.

I began to run as Swope finally lifted his horse to a trot. In the semidarkness, the footing was uncertain, and twice I fell over some obstacle that I had failed to see. Each time he gained a little more ground. The second time I got up from where I'd fallen, he was out of sight.

But his direction had been constant for the last few minutes and I would probably be safe in assuming that it would stay that way. I ran on, my breath growing short, a kind of desperation touching me.

Killing Shavano might be the incident that would touch off the whole bloody business. It might be the last push the homesteaders needed to make them fight back actively. They had been near that point earlier today and Father had stopped them then. This time there would be no stopping them.

My lungs were burning and it seemed as though I'd never get my breath again. A man that rides every place he goes is not usually capable of either sustained walking or running and I was no exception. But tonight I couldn't stop for breath. Time was slipping away too fast.

I heard Swope call out to Shavano and at the same time crested a little rise of ground and saw Shavano's wagon and fire ahead. The fire flickered faintly, almost three hundred yards away.

Swope sat his horse arrogantly at its edge. Then Shavano climbed down out of his canvas-covered wagon and stood there facing Swope.

He carried a rifle, but he held it loosely in his right hand, its muzzle pointing down. The two seemed to be talking but I couldn't hear anything—no words, no sounds. I was making too much noise myself.

The distance dwindled to two hundred yards and still I ran on. If I'd had a rifle I would have stopped, and perhaps shot Swope's horse out from under him. But two hundred yards is an impossible range for a revolver. If I hit anything at that range it would be a miracle.

Swope dismounted deliberately and for several moments more they talked. I had narrowed the distance now to a hundred yards and I could go no more. I stopped, dragging breath into my lungs with hoarse and rasping sounds. In an instant, when I had the breath for it, I would shout, and they both would turn and perhaps the dangerous moment would have passed.

But I never shouted because what happened then happened much too fast. One instant Shavano was standing there talking to Swope, the rifle hanging negligently at his side. The next he was falling.

Swope's draw was like lightning and he fired three times in rapid succession. He holstered the gun before Shavano even struck the ground and stood watching him.

Shavano had doubled slightly as the first bullet struck him. The second and third might have missed for all the effect they seemed to have, yet I knew at that range Swope couldn't possibly have missed. In a slightly doubled position he struck the ground and rolled onto his side. He lay there, still, in a curled position like a hibernating bear.

I yelled, "Swope! You son of a bitch!" and began to run again, hauling out my gun as I did. I wouldn't have had a chance with him just then, out of breath, shaking from both fatigue and shock. He'd have killed me as quickly, as efficiently and as easily as he had killed Shavano.

He turned, surprise in his face. He reached for his horse's reins, swung to the animal's back and rode out of the circle of firelight. From the darkness he yelled, "Tell your old man it was self-defense. He had a gun in his hand and he started to bring it up——"

I howled, "You goddam liar!"

"Maybe you didn't see it, Kelso, but I did. I was a hundred yards closer to him than you. I'll be out at Fleur de Lis if your old man wants to hear my side of it."

"You came out here to kill Shavano."

Swope laughed. "Prove it in court, Kelso. Try provin' it in court. Shavano sent for me and I came to see what he wanted with me."

I stood there helplessly, raging. I had seen it all and I knew it wasn't self-defense. I also knew Shavano hadn't sent for him. But proving it would be something else.

The hoofs of Swope's horse drummed against the ground as he rode away.

I stumbled on. Perhaps Shavano wasn't dead. Maybe he could still be saved, if I could get him to Doc Steiner in town.

I ran into the circle of firelight and knelt at his side. I looked at the bloody, spreading stains on his chest.

Swope had hit him three times, once on the left side of the chest, once on the right a little higher up, and once in the belly. There was no saving Shavano. He was dead.

I stood up. Faintly, from the direction of the main homesteader camp, I could hear the murmur, the grumble of voices. No use in my staying here. In fact, if I was caught here they'd probably tear me to pieces before they even gave me a chance to explain.

A torch flickered back there on the rise of ground I had crested myself only minutes before. They had heard the shots and were coming to investigate. . . .

I ducked rapidly out of the circle of firelight, hoping they had not seen me yet. I walked swiftly at right angles to the line between the homesteader camp and myself. I heard them shouting. . . .

The torches split. They had seen me, then, and were trying to cut me off.

I began to trot. They were searching blindly and I knew they'd not be able to see beyond the torches' light. I doubted if they could have recognized me in no more than a few seconds' time, at a distance of three hundred yards or more.

I trotted on and after I had gone a quarter mile, I turned toward town. I slowed to a walk before I entered it and let my breathing become normal again.

That stupid Swope! To him, killing was the solution to anything. Only in this case, killing was the worst thing he could have done. Until tonight, none of the homesteaders had been killed. Now one of them had. Now a reasonable solution of the problem was impossible.

I hurried along until I reached the plaza and crossed hurriedly to the sheriff's office, in which a lamp now burned.

The door was open. Father was sitting on a bench outside the door. Across the plaza at the Diablo, the cowman crowd had thinned but there were still several horses tied outside the place.

I said, "Swope just killed Shavano."

That brought him up straight on the bench. "What?"

"I saw it. After I brought you your supper, I saw him leave the Diablo and get on his horse. I figured that was kind of fishy so I followed him. He rode out to Shavano's wagon at the edge of the homesteader camp and shot him."

"A fight? A fair fight?"

I laughed bitterly, watching him closely. "No fight at all. They were talking and Swope shot him."

"You talk to Swope afterward?"

"At a distance. He said to tell you it was self-defense. Said Shavano started to raise his gun."

"Oh. Shavano had a gun?"

"A rifle. It was hanging at his side in his right hand. Swope could have killed half a dozen men while he was bringing it to bear. And he never tried. I was watching and I know."

Father scowled. "And you think I should go out and bring Swope in?"

"Don't you think so?" I stared at him in amazement.

"Maybe. Maybe not. I don't know yet."

"Well, you'd better make up your mind pretty soon. Because they'll be here pretty soon demanding that you do." My voice sounded cold and disapproving, even in my own ears.

He stared coldly at me. "It's simple to you, isn't it?"

I said, "Fairly simple. You're here to enforce the law. Swope just broke it."

He corrected me. "I'm here to keep the peace. There's a difference. If the Big Four and the homesteaders tangle, there's going to be more than one dead man lying around. I'm trying to keep that from happening."

I wondered if he was making excuses to himself as I asked, "Then why don't you send for troops?"

"Because troops would mean that the homesteaders

win the whole damned pot. And I'm not sure they should. The cowmen have some rights. They settled this land when nobody else wanted it and fought for every damned acre of it. If I can keep things from blowing up and keep the troops away, maybe the two sides will find a solution that's fair to both of them."

"Or maybe you'll get your head blown off." In spite of my doubts, my tone was more temperate now. When I'd come home he was stitting back with his bottle, letting the cowmen have it all their own way. This, at least, was an improvement over that. And this morning . . .

In the end nobody would praise him. Nobody would agree that what he'd done was the best that could be done. He'd get no thanks from anyone.

But at least he was trying now. At least he was fighting and that was more than he'd been doing two days ago.

16

We did not have long to wait. This time, however, the homesteaders came neither in a crowd nor in a mob. They came in a tight little group of seven thin-lipped, angry men.

Not one of them was like Shavano. These were older men than he and appeared to be responsible men with families who wanted only what the government had offered them, a hundred and sixty acres to live upon.

They entered the office and glared at my father for

several moments. Finally one of them, stocky, attired in a tight-fitting, shiny black suit, said, "Do you know what has happened, sheriff?"

Father said, "Suppose you tell me, Mr. MacIntosh."

"Shavano's been killed. Murdered."

My father nodded. "I know."

This brought their instant attention to me. They all stared at me suspiciously, then back at Father again.

"I suppose you know who did it too."

"I do."

"Then why are you here? Why aren't you out pursuing him?"

"Shavano had a gun in his hand, didn't he?"

Macintosh's eyes widened almost imperceptibly. "How do you know all this?"

"Martin was there when it happened."

They turned their attention to me again, with no less suspicion. "It was you we saw at Shavano's wagon?"

I nodded.

"Why did you run if you didn't kill him?"

I looked at him pityingly. "Would you have listened to anything I had to say?"

"We might, if you'd given us a chance."

"The same kind of chance you had this morning? To string me up or drag me behind a horse?"

MacIntosh looked away, a dull flush creeping into his face. After a moment's hesitation he said, "You saw the killer, then."

"I saw him."

"Who was it?"

144

I glanced at my father, then back at MacIntosh. I asked sourly, "You want to string him up too? Or would dragging do?"

He flushed more darkly, but this time his eyes sparkled with anger.

I said, "He's claiming self-defense. Claims Shavano raised his gun."

"That would be a point for a jury to decide. Are you going to arrest him, sheriff, or are you not?"

My father said coldly, "I'm going to do what I was elected to do, Mr. MacIntosh. I'm going to keep the peace. I'm going to arrest lawbreakers on my own discretion and file whatever charges seem warranted under the circumstances. I'm not going to follow your instructions or those of anyone else. Is that clear to you? I won't have my actions dictated."

"Unless it would be by your cowmen friends." MacIntosh was as angry as father was.

Father said icily, "I'll give you a choice, Mr. MacIntosh. Either apologize for that remark or get your damned carcass out of my office!"

MacIntosh's eyes flared violently. But he grumbled reluctantly, "Sorry, sheriff."

Father stared harshly at the other six. "Anybody else got anything to say?"

One bearded man nearly as tall as I, standing behind MacIntosh, said, "We can assume, then, that you intend to do nothing at all about Shavano's murder. Is that correct?"

"It is not correct. I intend to investigate Shavano's

death as thoroughly as is possible. If the facts warrant it, I will arrest the killer and hold him for trial. But I will not tell you his name so that you can take the law into your own hands."

"What about the men out at Cactus Springs? Do you reckon they're going to claim self-defense too? Maybe they'll just say Satterlee attacked them."

Father said softly, "Get out of here. The bunch of you."

The same voice said insistently, "And how about the next one of us that gets dragged or killed? It appears to me, sheriff, that you're scared to arrest anyone. Why? Is someone threatening you? Are the cowmen threatening your son for killing Link unless you—"

He got no chance to finish. Father seized him by the arm, whirled him around and marched him out the door. He gave the man a push that sent him staggering across the puncheon walk. I'd seen him treat a quarrelsome drunk the same way many a time before I'd gone away.

The others hurried out behind him, walked around him and stood again in a group facing him from the street.

MacIntosh said angrily, "You're going to be sorry, sheriff. Because you're wrong. We're not a blight or a pestilence. We're here to stay. We've come to inherit the land. There is right on our side, and if that isn't enough, the United States government is on our side as well."

Father didn't answer him. There wasn't, after all,

very much that he could say. MacIntosh was right and Father was beginning to suspect he was—at least about the homesteaders having come to inherit the land. The Indians hadn't been able to stand up against both the cowmen and the government, then backing them. Now the cowmen were about to be driven out just as they had driven the Indians out.

Father said wearily, "Go on back to your camps."

The men glared at him with sullen anger, then turned and stalked away toward the cottonwoods. Father came back into the office. He snorted disgustedly, then fished in his vest pocket for a cigar, which he lighted with impatient, angry motions. He puffed several times before he said, "When you settle down, for God's sake be something besides a lawman. Get a job where everything's either black or white."

I said, "Neither side intends to give an inch, do they?"

"Hell, no, they don't! And that's all it would take. A little reasonableness on both sides and there wouldn't have to be a fight."

Death struggle would have been a better term than fight, I thought. The trouble was, Father was filling, or trying to fill, a larger role than that of sheriff. He was trying to be the courts as well.

Swift and impartial justice would do a lot to ease the tensions here. If the cowmen knew that every act of violence would be met with instant action on the part of the sheriff's office to bring the perpetrators to trial, acts of violence would virtually stop happening. And if the homesteaders could rely on the protection of the sheriff's office, they would be less likely to resort to violence themselves.

A new order had come, or was coming, to this land I knew so well. In the past, Father had often filled both roles—those of sheriff and judge. He had even filled the role of executioner. He was finding it hard to change, but he had to change or die.

I stared at him thoughtfully, wondering how much he was being influenced by McGann's threat against me. And I realized how little I really knew of him. He was an impassive giant, a rock, a legend that would be remembered long after his earthly presence had been committed to the ground. But his grief over my mother's death had taught me that he was a man as well, who felt deeply about many things even though he never showed his feelings to another living soul.

Mother, had she been living, would have known whether he was being influenced by McGann's threat or whether he was not. I simply couldn't know because I didn't know my father well enough.

I said, "Going to arrest Jess Swope?"

"Probably. But he'll keep. He's not going to run away."

I said, "That's not the point. I think what the homesteaders need just now is an expression of good faith. Arresting Swope would be that to them. Besides, you know he murdered Shavano. I told you so."

"You were a hundred yards away."

I said, my own anger stirring, "You're straddling the

fence. You're not taking any stands you don't have to take. And you're only making things worse."

He glared at me. "And you're a kid that's hardly dry behind the ears. Run against me next election time."

I felt the blood drain from my face. I said stubbornly, "There'll be a sodbuster sheriff next election time."

We were both furious. Outside it was fully dark and it was quiet in the streets, but the quiet was unnatural and ominous. Therefore the rattle and creak of an approaching wagon was loud and heard by both of us all the way across the square.

I turned and walked to the door. I felt presumptuous for having tried to tell Father how to do his job. I was confused between pride and shame. This morning I had been very proud of the way he faced the mob outside in the sunny street. Now I was ashamed because he refused to do anything about Swope.

Yet his curt suggestion that I run against him next election time made me realize that I'd do no better than he, indeed that I wouldn't do as well.

A homesteader was approaching. His wagon was loaded high, apparently with everything he owned. Behind it trailed a team of work horses and a cow. Beside him on the seat a woman sat, a squalling baby in her arms. From tears in the canvas, the faces of children peered. There must have been six of them at least, jammed in amongst the wagon's load.

He pulled up in front, tied the reins and climbed down. He marched across the gallery.

I stepped aside to let him enter. I was so used to all

149

of my father's visitors being angry that it didn't surprise me to see that this one also was.

He flung a scrap of paper at my father furiously. "There! There is another one. I'm not staying here any longer. The lives of my family mean more to me than a piece of land. If you were a man—if you were fit to wear that star on your vest—I would not have to leave!" He stopped, breathing hard as though he had been running or walking fast.

He was a heavy-featured man, shorter than I by several inches. His head was bald except for tufts of graying hair above his ears. He wore farmer's overalls and heavy work shoes that were covered with dried mud. He wore a blue Union cavalry trooper's shirt, carefully mended so many times that it almost seemed like a patchwork quilt.

Father didn't even glance at the paper on the floor. I knew he'd never pick it up. He had a very good idea of what was written there and who had written it.

I walked over and picked it up. It was crumpled but I spread it out and read: "NINETY-FIVE HOMESTEADERS WERE ALL THAT TARRIED. ONE BY ONE THEY'LL ALL BE BURIED."

I handed the paper to him. I said, "We both know who wrote that. We both know he ought to be in jail. Why isn't he?"

"Later, Martin. Later." He glanced at the angry homesteader. He said, "I can't stop you from leaving any more than I could keep you from coming here. Do what you think you have to do."

150

The man said disgustedly, "Law! You don't even know the meaning of the word!"

He turned and stalked from the office. I watched while he climbed to the seat, untied the reins and shouted the team into motion. Without turning I said, "This morning I was proud of you. For the first time since I came home, I was proud of you. But I'm not proud now." I swung around and faced him angrily. "And don't waste your breath telling me I don't know what I'm talking about or that I'm just a kid. I know what's right and wrong. I know damned good and well that if you'd take a stand—not for either side but for the law you're supposed to represent—there wouldn't be any trouble. They'd learn to settle their differences peacefully if you'd get up out of your chair and do your job."

His jaw hung slack with surprise. My hands were shaking, both from anger and from defying my own father. I said, "Everybody in this country has to know that they'll be held accountable by you for everything they do. You've got to start with that bunch that was out at Cactus Springs. I'll give you most of their names. Then you've got to go get Swope. And every damned time someone breaks the peace you've got to go after him."

He yelled, "Shut up! Don't you talk to me like that!"

I yelled back, "I won't shut up. It's time somebody talked to you exactly like that! I'm not afraid of their goddam threats. Let them bring me to trial if that's what they've got to do. But don't let worrying about me ruin the whole damned country and you and me along with it."

He crossed the room to me. His face was white with rage. His hands were clenched into fists. I braced myself. He'd probably hit me now and I knew I could never hit him back. Maybe I deserved it too. I didn't know. All I did know was I wasn't sorry for what I'd said. I'd meant every word of it. I'd say all the same things again.

I said, "Hit me, damn it! Go ahead. But you won't shut me up that way. And you won't stop what I've said from going around in your head because you know I'm right. Swope ought to be lying back there in a cell right now. So should those others that were out at Cactus Springs. So should every damn man that breaks the law, no matter which side he belongs to."

Watching him, I saw something begin to crumble in his face and this made me even madder than his bull-headedness and anger had. I said, "And don't crawl back into that bottle either. Mother's dead and all the whiskey in the Goddamned world isn't going to bring her back. You raised me to act like a man. Now act like one yourself."

He hit me then, with his clenched fist and squarely on the jaw. My feet left the floor and I flew back halfway across the room.

My shoulders struck the solid adobe wall with an impact that made me think I had broken them. I slid down the wall in a shower of dry adobe dust and whitewash.

Not quite out, I stared up at him. His eyes were blazing, his mouth set grimly, his face white with the most terrible rage I had ever seen in him. If I hadn't been his son, I know he would have killed me outright.

I tried to move and couldn't. I could see but I seemed to be numbed and couldn't feel. It was as though my head were the only living part of me.

He tried to speak, choked on his own rage, swallowed and roared, "Don't you ever talk to me like that again!"

My own voice seemed to come from far away. "Why not? I'm not a little boy any more. I'm grown and I can think for myself. And next time you hit me like that I'm going to knock your damned block off!"

I struggled to my feet, swayed and almost fell. I stared at him defiantly and said, "Want me to say it again? Because I still mean every word."

We stood there glaring at each other for what seemed an eternity. Of one thing I was sure. He wouldn't hit me again without getting hit in return. Maybe he was tougher than I and maybe he could beat the living hell out of me, but I didn't intend to make it easy for him. Next time he'd have to work for it.

Mother had said I was like him and I hoped she had been right. Apparently she had been right, both about that and about the need for me to go away awhile. By going, I seemed to have found the courage to stand up to him, and I never had before. But I hoped it didn't have to end in a knock-down-drag-out fight between us, because if it did nothing would ever quite be the same again. He wouldn't be able to forgive me, nor I him.

It didn't end that way. His face began to soften reluctantly. His mouth relaxed and color began to return to his face. His eyes became less hard and at last his mouth was touched with a spare, unwilling smile.

I said, "Are we going out to Fleur de Lis?"

The grin faded. "Telling me what to do?"

I said, "I don't know how she lived with you, as bullheaded as you are."

The grin came back, a real grin now. He said, "Let's go."

17

The rare moments of closeness with my father are among the fondest memories I have. Riding out to Fleur de Lis was one of those few times when we seemed to both understand and like each other and the hostility between us, while it might return, was at least gone for the present.

Yet a cloud was in my thoughts—of worry, of foreboding. This would not be an easy thing—riding into Fleur de Lis at night to arrest a man like Swope. And if that wasn't enough, we were going to bring in the men responsible for the business out at Cactus Springs.

If Father thought of the difficulties, and I am sure he did, he didn't mention them. He rode along at a steady, bone-jolting trot, a gait that is easiest of all on the horse and one he rode without any visible discomfort. Occasionally he would speak, nostalgically mentioning something that had happened years ago. But mostly he rode in silence that was companionable and pleasant because of the closeness of our thoughts.

I was glad I had come back and glad I had stayed. Nothing, I was sure, would work out exactly as I wished it to, but then nothing ever does. At least I was home, with those I loved, and if tragedy came to us we would meet it together, and overcome it, and go on from there.

The thought that my father might be hurt or killed was like a knife twisting in my side. The thought that I might be hurt or killed did not even occur to me.

Montour's place was not as far as McGann's, and we bore right of the course we would have taken to reach The Sentinel. It must have been close to nine when we brought the place into sight.

Lights blazed from the windows of the house, and from the bunkhouse too.

Fleur de Lis was built entirely of adobe, even to the corrals. A scattered hodgepodge of buildings it was, that had grown in direct proportion to the growth of the cattle herd. You could still see, in daylight, the part of the great, sprawlling house that had been Montour's original one-room adobe shack. The rest had been added on, a room or two at a time, until the result, incredibly ugly, sprawled like a huge, hungry spider on the face of the grassland.

On all sides of it adobe outbuildings squatted—none

at right angles with the others, but each serving the purpose for which it had been built.

In the middle of the house several cottonwoods grew up, shading it in summer, breaking the bitter sweep of wind in winter. Rather than destroy the trees they had simply built the house around them. And roughly in the center of the house there was a court-yard or patio that had always reminded me of the spider's mouth.

As we approached, Father said, "All right. Tell me their names."

I said, "Dugan, LeBlanc, Reilly, Shane. Two others that I don't know. They weren't here when I went away."

"But you'd know 'em."

"I'd know them."

He said, "All right, let's go in. We'll take Swope and the four you named and let the others go until later."

He lifted his horse to a gallop. I stayed immediately beside him and we galloped through the gate to pull up in the center of the courtyard beside the well in a rolling cloud of dust.

I grinned inwardly. No slipping in timidly for Father. He might not have much of a hand, but he sure as hell was going to bet it like aces.

He roared, "Montour! You here?"

I waited until he swung to the ground and then immediately followed suit. We stepped away from our horses and stood together facing the main entrance of the house.

156

There was light in the courtyard, from lanterns hanging on both sides of the main door, from smaller lanterns hanging along the covered gallery that went all the way around the courtyard. The huge plank door opened and Montour stood framed in it. Behind him I could see Swope, and Swope's wife, and several other women I did not recognize.

Without looking around I knew the entrance to the courtyard had been closed by Montour's crew, who had come to watch the fun.

I felt trapped. If they refused to surrender Swope, or the men I had named . . . Father didn't seem concerned or if he was it didn't show. He said harshly, "I want Dugan, LeBlanc, Reilly, Shane. The charge is arson and if you need 'em you can see Judge Perkins about bail. I want Swope for murder. I want all five of 'em right now."

Montour stepped outside. Swope followed, pushing his wife and the other women back and closing the door behind him. The pair walked slowly across the cobblestone courtyard toward us, their boot-heels and spurs ringing against its hard surface.

Behind us a man coughed and I saw Father stiffen slightly. More than ever, in this instant, Fleur de Lis seemed like a spider crouched upon the grass. And I felt very much like a fly entangled in its web.

Montour and Swope approached until they were less than a dozen feet away.

Montour was French, descended from French Canadian trappers who had settled in Canada in the early days. It explained his use of a fleur-de-lis as a brand. He was short, and broad, and wore a small goatee, but whatever accent his forebears might have had was gone altogether from his speech.

He said coldly, "John Kelso, you are a Goddamned fool if you think I'm going to give them up."

"And you're a worse fool if you think I'm going back without 'em."

"You're threatening to shoot it out with me? Are you crazy, man?"

"Crazy? I'm the law. I'm putting Swope and those other four under arrest. Makes no difference to me, Montour, whether I take 'em in dead or alive. But I'm going to take 'em in."

Swope said mockingly, "There are twenty men behind you, sheriff. And they've all got guns."

Father stared hard at him. "If they use 'em, they'll be charged with obstructing an officer in the performance of his duties. If they're alive to be charged with anything. Unbuckle your gun belt, Swope. Send someone to saddle a horse for you."

Swope swaggered toward us. He stopped. He said contemptuously, "Kelso, you go straight to hell!"

I didn't glance aside at Father's face. I was watching Montour. And I was very conscious of all those guns at our backs.

Besides, I didn't need to look at him. I knew he wasn't going to leave without making his arrest. Nobody had ever bluffed him yet and they weren't going to succeed at it now. I knew, and he did, and every man here knew too that if Father backed down it was the end of law in this part of New Mexico. That, I suppose, was what Swope was working toward.

Father turned his head slightly. "Dugan, LeBlanc, Reilly and Shane. Get your horses saddled and be ready to go."

As far as I could tell, nobody back there moved. Father took a deliberate step toward Swope. I knew without being told that he was counting on me to keep my eyes glued to Montour and to forestall any action he might be tempted to take.

Facing Swope, Father said in evenly measured tones, "Jess, you are a murderin' yellow dog. It isn't in you to draw your gun against a man you know is as fast as you. You shoot men in the back, or from ambush, and if you haven't unbuckled that gun belt in ten seconds I'm going to shoot you right in the belly where it will hurt the most."

My right hand was tense. I wanted to look at Swope and see how he had taken that but my eyes didn't leave Montour. I took a step to the right and said softly, "Stay out of it, Montour. It's between the two of them."

There was silence after that and it seemed to last for years. It was broken by my father's roar, so unexpected and so loud that every man in the courtyard must have started violently. I know I did. "Damn you, unbuckle that belt! Right now!"

Perhaps Swope would have done it had not a diversion occurred. Behind Montour the door opened and a

159

woman's voice shrilled, "Jess! Are you all right?"

It was Montour's daughter, the one who was married to Swope. What she saw in him I'll never know but it was obvious that she thought more of him than he deserved.

Perhaps he did not want her to see him back down. Perhaps her shrill voice only broke the hypnotic, compelling effect of my father's demand.

Swope moved like light and I caught the blur of it from a corner of my eye. I heard Swope's gun roar and my father's, so close together that they were scarcely distinguishable one from the other. My own gun was in my hand, hammer back, finger tight against the trigger as Montour's gun cleared leather. I put a bullet into the ground at his feet and bawled hoarsely, "Hold it! Next one goes right between your eyes."

He froze, the gun dangling from his right hand. I yelled, "Drop it on the ground!"

He dropped it. I wanted to look at my father. Terror was an icy hand in my chest and I had to see if he was still on his feet. But I didn't dare look. Not now.

Without turning, I shouted, "The rest of you back there! Drop your belts and come this way. Line up on the gallery with your backs to me. Try shooting me if you want. But I'll get Montour sure before I fall."

Montour growled, "Do what he said, damn it! He can kill me before one of you can knock him down."

I heard the thud of belts falling. Then I heard the soft shuffle of their boots, the occasional tinkle of a spur. I began to pace right, a careful step at a time. After a dozen steps I was beside Montour and slightly behind.

Only then did I dare look to see what had happened between my father and Swope.

Father stood like a rock, like The Sentinel towering behind Mike McGann's big house. His gun was in his hand and a thin plume of smoke drifted away from the muzzle of it.

Swope stood facing him, just as he had before. But Swope's gun was neither in his holster nor in his hand. It was on the cobblestones. With his right hand he was holding his left arm above the elbow. Blood leaked redly through his fingers and dripped steadily to the paving beneath his feet.

Father said with even coldness, "Now, damn you, tell someone to saddle up your horse!"

Swope's voice was thin with pain. "Get him, Milo."

Milo stared at me from the gallery. "All right with you?"

I nodded. "Get horses for the other four too."

Milo hurried away, a grizzled oldster with a white, scared face. I watched him go and all I could think was: We brought it off! Damn them, we brought it off! Yet I couldn't stop, nor could I account for the feeling of disaster that had crept over me.

The feeling made me more watchful. The women came running out from the house and Montour sent them back harshly, his voice like the crack of a whip. Both Father and I stood as though frozen there in the courtyard at Montour's Fleur de Lis, waiting for the horses to be brought in.

161

It took awhile. It must have taken ten minutes. We should have sent others to help, I thought, yet I knew as well that sending more would have been reckless. More than one . . . They might have been tempted to get rifles and turn the tables on us.

Milo came at last, leading five horses through the courtyard gate. Father didn't speak; he seemed to be almost in a trance. So I said, "All right, Swope. Mount up. You others mount up too. But leave your reins on the ground."

This could still blow up in our faces. One man with a hold-out gun . . .

I watched them intently as they walked to the horses and mounted up. I said, "Milo. The sheriff will lead Swope's horse. Tie the other four together, reins to tail, then tie the string to the tail of Swope's horse."

Milo moved among the horses, following my instructions. Father walked to his horse and swung ponderously to the saddle. Milo stared at him a moment, then picked up the reins of Swope's horse, led the animal to him and handed him the reins.

I know, I understood now my feeling of disaster. Father had been hit. He had stayed on his feet and he might stay in the saddle until we left the courtyard, perhaps even until we reached the town. But only his great, iron will was keeping him erect. He was hit badly and there was no time to lose.

None of the others seemed to know so far. Except Milo, who had understood Father's inability to bend and pick up the reins of Jess Swope's horse.

162

Father moved away, riding deliberately and slowly toward the courtyard gate. I stayed where I was until he and the horses he trailed behind him cleared it and disappeared into the darkness beyond. I said harshly, "Don't get any ideas about coming after us. Not if you want Jess to go to trial."

I rode out then, wanting to spur my horse and race away in Father's wake. I controlled the impulse and paced him at a deliberate walk until I was well clear of the gate. Then I sank my spurs in deep.

Within two minutes I had overhauled the six. I rode to the head of the column. I asked softly, "How bad are you hit?"

It was almost half a minute before he answered me and when he did his voice was soft with pain. "Bad enough. But I'll make it to town."

"Bleeding bad?"

"Inside, I think. Not much outside."

I said, "To hell with these prisoners. Let them go. Then let me tie you up and go after a buckboard while you rest."

"No!" His voice was strong and implacable. "No, by God!"

I didn't argue with him. It would do no good. If I wanted him to dismount and lie down I'd have to fight him first.

My belly like ice, I dropped back to the tail of the column. During the next couple of hours I prayed more than I had ever prayed in all my life before.

18

It was the longest ride I had ever made, that one from Fleur de Lis to town. The seconds seemed like hours, the hours like days. Father kept his horse at a steady walk, a smooth gait on Father's horse but a rough, hard gait for a man with internal wounds. I knew the incredible pain he must be enduring even though he never made a sound.

Swope and the other four rode in sullen silence. I had kept my voice low when I spoke to Father about his wound, and his answering voice had been soft with pain. I doubted if Swope knew yet that he was wounded and I hoped he did not find out. He could cause trouble if he did—by spurring or kicking his horse, by making it difficult for Father to control the string. Damn him, I thought. If he tried anything like that, I'd shoot him down.

My eyes burned and my throat felt choked. All my life my father had been a giant, indestructible as the ageless rock of The Sentinel. Now, suddenly, he had become mortal. He was hurt badly and might die. And as I faced the probability of his death in my thoughts, I knew suddenly, for the first time, how very much he meant to me and how much we were alike.

It must have been close to midnight when I saw the few dim lights of Rio de Oro ahead. A few minutes later we were threading our way through its crooked streets.

In front of the jail he stopped. I rode immediately to the head of the column, drawing my gun. I said, "Stay mounted, Pa. I'll lock 'em up."

He didn't protest but sat silent and unmoving on his horse while I had the five prisoners dismount and herded them inside. I made Reilly light the lamp and, carrying it, herded them into the rear and locked them up.

From behind the bars, Swope chortled triumphantly, "I got him, didn't I?" He was obviously in pain himself and much weakened by loss of blood.

I wanted to open the cell door, go in and beat the hell out of him, but I controlled myself and didn't even reply.

His voice changed and became a whine. "You'd let a man bleed to death, wouldn't you? Get Doc Steiner over here."

I stared at him coldly. "Doc Steiner's going to look at the sheriff first. If you haven't bled to death by then I'll send him back here."

Carrying the lamp, I went up front and slammed the barred connecting door. I put the lamp down on the desk and went outside.

Father still sat on his horse but he had slumped forward and was holding onto the horn with both hands. I said, "How do you figure it will be easiest to get you down?"

He growled hoarsely, "Ain't no easy way. Just help me off and get me inside."

I went to his horse and put up my hands. He slid off

toward me, so heavily I thought he would knock me down. But I managed to stay upright and break his fall. I got my arms around him and half carrying, half dragging, got him into the office.

I stopped to rest just inside the door, then helped him across the room to the office couch and laid him down.

He went out cold when he hit the couch. His face was bathed with sweat and had turned a peculiar greenish shade. I glanced at his abdomen and saw the stain of darkened blood on his shirt.

I turned and hurried out. I leaped astride his horse and pounded recklessly up the street.

Pray God, I thought, that Doc Steiner isn't out treating a homesteader the way he had been the night my mother died. I thundered up the silent streets until I reached his house and I swung to the ground, running, before the horse could stop.

I beat thunderously on the heavy door with the butt of my gun. It wasn't more than half a minute before I heard his outraged yell. "Damn it, stop that racket! You trying to beat down the door?"

I yelled back, "Then get your pants on and get out here! The sheriff's been shot. If he dies . . ."

I heard nothing more from inside but within half a minute the door banged open and Doc appeared, trying to button his shirt with one hand while he carried his bag with the other. I took the bag and he finished buttoning his shirt and tucked it in.

I said, "Use the horse. I'll follow on foot."

He grunted something I didn't catch and mounted Father's horse. I handed up the bag and he thundered away to be lost instantly in the pitch darkness of the street.

I ran along in the dusty wake he made. It seemed to take me forever but I reached the jail before the dust he raised had stopped settling. I ran inside.

He had Father's shirt cut away and was looking at the wound. He said, "Get me hot water and towels. Hurry!"

I went to the potbellied office stove and shook the ashes down. I built a fire with hands that trembled, a big fire, and I opened the damper wide. I filled a big pan with water and put it on the stove. Then I hurried out and down the street toward home.

It was dark and Francisca was in bed. I bawled, "Francisca! Get up and get dressed and come down to the office. Father's been shot!"

I snatched up all the towels I could find and ran out again. I returned to the office. Inside there was a strong smell of whiskey. Doc was bent over my father, a surgeon's knife in his hand. Lacking water, he had washed his hands and the wound itself with whiskey. He grunted, "What the hell took you so long? Come hold him down!"

I went over and put my weight on Father's shoulders to hold them down. A moment later Francisca came in and Doc Steiner said, "Hold his legs down, woman."

I didn't watch what Doc did. I couldn't, I knew, without getting sick. But I was conscious of all the blood. There must have been a gallon of it on the couch, on Doc Steiner's hands and arms, and on the floor.

My lips moved and I prayed constantly and silently. Francisca was praying too, in Spanish.

Doc turned and seized a towel. He dried the blood on his hands and arms, then went into his bag for surgical needles and catgut sutures to close the wound.

I looked at my father's face. That awful greenish pallor was still in it. The eyes were closed, the breathing scarcely audible. I had the awful premonition that he was going to die.

If he did. . . . My throat almost closed. If he died, I would go back there in that cell and kill Swope with my own bare hands.

Doc sutured the incision he had made. He made a pad from one of the towels, soaked it with whiskey and laid it gently on the wound. He ripped a sheet I had brought with the towels into strips and made a roll of the strips. Then he said, "Raise him a little while I bandage him."

Francisca raised his hips, I his chest. Doc rolled the bandage around and around his midsection over the wound and the whiskey-soaked compress.

He finished and we eased Father down. Doc got the washpan off the shelf, dipped out some hot water from the pan on the stove and crossed the room to the washstand against the wall. He washed his hands and arms, leaving the wash water opaque with my father's blood. He dried on a clean towel and looked at me.

His expression was as empty as that of a poker player holding a flush. I asked, "What kind of chance has he got?"

"Not much. I got the bullet out and I got most of the blood out of his abdomen. But if he's moved . . . it'll start him bleeding all over again. Next time it'll finish him."

"Then he's got to stay right where he is."

Doc Steiner nodded, "And the county's without a sheriff just when it needs him most."

"To hell with that." But I didn't mean it. I knew being sheriff was not a light thing with Father, to be lightly brushed aside. He had spent his life, a good part of it at least, wearing the star right here in Rio de Oro.

I said, "He swore me in as deputy before he passed out." It was a lie but nobody was going to know the difference. I looked straight at Doc as I said the words, then added, "Take a look at Swope, will you?"

I went back with him and let him in Swope's cell. I watched while he dressed the flesh wound in Swope's arm. Then I locked the cell again and followed Doc back to the office. He began to put things away in his bag. "I'll look in first thing in the morning. Meantime, watch him pretty close. He could get delirious and start thrashing around or trying to get up."

Francisca said brokenly, "I stay with him, *señor.* He not get up or move around."

Doc nodded. "You know where I'll be if you need me." He went out and trudged down the walk toward home.

I went over and stared down at my father on the couch. Lying helpless this way, his tremendous personality submerged, he seemed less a giant than ever before. His breathing came in hoarse gusts, uneven and irregular. His face was covered with sweat and he was beginning to shiver as though from cold.

I picked up a towel and wiped his face carefully. I said, "He should have some blankets over him."

"*Si señor.* I will get them."

"No. You stay here. You'll probably be better with him if anything goes wrong than I would. I'll get the blankets."

I looked down at Father's face for a moment more, then turned and went outside, wondering if he would still be alive when I returned. The horses we had brought the prisoners on were still tied together, reins to tail. I went from one to another of them, unsaddling and turning them loose. They'd go back out to Fleur de Lis, I knew.

I picked up the reins of Father's horse and my own and led them down the street. Reaching our house, I put them into the stable, where I unsaddled, watered and fed them both. After that I crossed toward the house.

In the darkness I had not noticed the saddle horse in the courtyard, but I noticed him now. And I noticed too the saddle he wore—a sidesaddle.

I stopped suddenly, frowning to myself. Sue? I shook my head. Sue wouldn't ride a sidesaddle unless she was all dressed up for a dance or something and

170

then she'd probably drive a buggy instead. Laura, then. But what the hell was she doing here in the middle of the night?

I went into the house, which was dark except for the single lamp burning dimly in the kitchen. I smelled her perfume as I entered and saw her at the same time.

She sat sat huddled at the table, her head down on her arms. She raised it as I came in and looked at me with brimming eyes and a mouth that trembled violently. "Oh, Martin, I'm so glad you're here!"

I said, "You'll have to wait. Father's been shot and he needs blankets. I'll take them down and then come back."

She started to protest but I didn't listen to her. I gathered up an armload of blankets and went back out again.

I scowled all the way to the sheriff's office. What the hell did Laura want of me now? Whatever it was, she had certainly picked a poor time to come to me with it. I had a jail full of prisoners and my father was hovering near to death. I knew the arrest of the five wouldn't go unchallenged long by the cowman crowd.

I reached the jail and took the blankets inside. Father still lay on the office couch, just as he had been when I left. I gave the blankets to Francisca, said, "I'll be right back," and went out the door again.

I could not help feeling impatient with Laura and angry because she had come to me in the middle of the night. Good God, what if Mike McGann discovered she was here?

I reached the house again, but this time before I went inside I led Laura's horse to the stable and put him in one of the stalls. I left the saddle on.

I heard her weeping before I reached the house and she sounded like a hurt or heartbroken child. But tonight the sound did not move me as it might have another time.

19

I stepped into the house and pulled the door closed behind me. Laura looked once at my face, then came running to throw herself into my arms. I held her awkwardly for a long time, waiting for her hysteria to subside. And as I did, something within me softened toward her. She was so helpless, so small . . . like some wild thing frightened half to death.

At last she quieted and pulled herself away. "I shouldn't bother you with my troubles, Martin. I have no right—"

I asked, "What's the matter? Maybe I can help."

"It's Mike. I'm afraid of him." She tugged her dress off one white shoulder to display two red welts. She blushed and rearranged the dress immediately.

I said, "What did he do that with?"

"A quirt. Oh, Martin, what am I going to do? I'm afraid he'll kill me next."

"What brought it on?" I tried not to think of Sue's accusations. Yet I couldn't forget the way Laura had been with me out in the kitchen of McGann's house.

172

"Nothing. Nothing, Martin, I swear it. One of the men came in to see when I expected Mike back from town. Mike saw him leaving and . . ."

I studied her face closely. If Mike had seen me leaving there early this morning . . . he'd have taken a shotgun to me and a quirt to Laura, and I wouldn't have blamed him much.

I wanted to believe her, and tried. Perhaps my own trouble, my own terrible worry about my father, kept desire for Laura from stirring in me right then. And without desire to obscure my judgment . . .

I asked, "What do you want to do?"

"I don't know." She seemed confused. "I'll have to leave him, I suppose. But I'm afraid to do that too."

I said, "I've known Mike McGann all my life. He might be violent if he was jealous, but he won't hurt you for trying to leave."

"Can I stay here with you tonight, Martin? Isn't there a woman here—so that people wouldn't talk?"

I said, "She's down at the jail with Pa. Hell, no, you can't stay here. Do you think I'm crazy? Mike will be looking for you and if he ever found you here . . ."

A strange expression touched her face, one that was almost hard. She said, "Then take me over to the hotel. I'm afraid to go alone."

I shrugged with relief. "All right. I guess I can do that much."

She walked hesitantly to the door and paused there with her hand on the knob. I couldn't rid myself of the thought that this was too easy. I hadn't expected her to

173

suggest the hotel. I'd been getting desperate, wondering how I was going to get her out of here. Now she was going and I was going with her and in a few minutes she'd be safe in the hotel and I could put her out of my thoughts.

I blew out the lamp and she opened the door. She stepped outside and I followed, closing the door behind.

Instantly I knew that something was very wrong. There was a horse in the courtyard that had not been there before. A man towered in the saddle, silent at first but unmistakable because of his size. It was Mike McGann.

For a second time since coming home I felt like a rube at the county fair.

I stood there frozen with surprise for what must have been half a minute. I saw the ponderous shape of the horse merge with the shadow as Mike dismounted, then separate again as Mike stepped away. He roared suddenly, "Damn you, Mart, start shooting! You'd better kill me quick too, because if you don't I'm going to blow your damn head off and that slut's too!"

I didn't even reach for my gun. I grabbed Laura with one hand, the door with the other. I flung her inside so violently that she staggered across the room, collided with the table and crashed to the floor. I leaped inside myself and banged the door shut behind me. I shot the bolt in place and stepped aside just as three bullets tore through the planks of the door.

I said softly, "God damn you, you knew he was right

behind you. You knew he'd be out there when you opened the door."

She began to whimper. "I didn't either. I swear I didn't, Martin! He must have followed me—"

"And you made sure he didn't lose you in the darkness, didn't you? What'd you want me to do, kill him for you so you could inherit the ranch?"

Her weeping became more intense. "I don't— know—how you can say such awful things to me!"

"Because I'm thinking straight instead of thinking about making love to you. Well, I'm not going to kill him for you. Not Mike McGann."

"Then what are you going to do?"

"I don't know yet." I didn't see what I could do. In order to get out of there I was going to have to kill Mike or let him kill me. And neither solution made any sense.

I said with cold fury, "You had it all figured out, didn't you? You got him all stirred up earlier and then you took off for town, making sure he saw you leave."

I was so angry I scarcely heard the window bang in my father's room and if I had noticed it I would have thought it was the wind. Laura had figured this out, all right, and as far as I could see she hadn't made a damn mistake. Mike had seen her with me. He knew she was in here. There would be no opportunity for explanations and even if there had been, Mike wouldn't have listened to them. There was only one way out, Laura had made sure of that. I had to face Mike McGann. I had to either kill him or be killed myself.

I stared at Laura, wondering how I could ever have wanted her. She was pretty, perhaps even beautiful, but it was purely a surface beauty and superficial. She was made in the shape of beauty but she was a bitch inside.

I don't know what made me look around but I did and there was Sue McGann standing in the doorway leading to my father's room. Her eyes were furious, her mouth compressed with anger. She was staring at Laura, not at me.

She said angrily, "This is cozy, isn't it?"

I said, "How did you get in here?"

"Your father's window. It opens onto the street and it wasn't fastened. From the look of things it's a good thing I did get in."

She glanced at me briefly and for an instant she reminded me of a she-lion I had come upon once in the mountains beyond The Sentinel. The lioness had cubs and thought I threatened them and she had looked much as Sue looked now.

I said, "It isn't a damned bit cozy and you can save the nasty remarks. Your father's outside and he swears he's either going to kill me or that I'm going to have to kill him."

"I know he's out there. She led him here. She was so darned careful not to lose him that she made it practically impossible for me to lose either one of them."

I glanced at Laura. I was appalled at the change in her and wondered for a second time how I could have come so close to losing my head over her. There was no beauty in either her face or her eyes right now.

She screeched, "You're a liar! Mike beat me with a quirt and I ran away from him. I didn't know where else to go so I came to Martin. You think he's yours, but he isn't. He's mine. I can—" She stopped and glanced at me. She must have seen something in my face that shocked her because she said, "Anyway, there's nothing he can do about it. Mike's outside and not in a mood to listen to explanations from anyone. Sooner or later Martin's going to have to go out or Mike will come in. And then I'll get the McGann Land and Cattle Company instead of you!"

I thought of Father lying down there in the sheriff's office close to death. I thought of the cells filled with prisoners. I had no business wasting time here. I ought to be down there with him and with the prisoners, seeing to it that nothing went wrong.

I could have gone out the same window through which Sue had come in, but even if I'd been able to do it, it wouldn't have solved anything. Mike would come to the sheriff's office after me and I'd have to face him there. No. Laura had won. There was nothing for it but to go out and face Mike McGann.

I looked at Sue. "Looks like she's right." I got up, reached for my holstered gun, then self-consciously let my hand fall away. I felt sick. How could I kill Sue's father? I knew the answer to that. I couldn't. While I was trying, he would kill me.

There was a sour kind of irony in this situation. The conflict between cowmen and homesteaders had been the burning issue, the one I had thought most explosive. Now I was about to be killed over a slut that had slept with every man who would sleep with her. And not because of anything I had done either.

I said, "Sue, at least make sure Mike knows what she is and how she maneuvered this. Make sure he gets rid of her."

"Mart! You can't go out there!" Whatever anger had been in her was gone. She ran to me and threw her arms around me as though she could hold me by force.

Suddenly then, so suddenly that I staggered against the wall, she released me. She ran toward Laura, my gun, which she had withdrawn from its holster, in her hand. I yelled, "Sue! No!"

But she didn't shoot Laura or even try. She swung the heavy gun at the side of Laura's head.

It connected glancingly. Laura slumped to the floor. A little trickle of blood sprang from a gash on her cheekbone and trickled across her white skin. I said, "What the hell good is that going to do?"

"You'll see. Come on." She tossed the gun on the table, grabbed my hand and pulled me toward the door. She whispered, "Go on out and talk to Mike."

She opened the door and pushed me out. He saw me, however dimly, and yelled, "Damn you, are you ready now?"

I said, "Mike, you're wrong about this."

"Wrong, am I? Why, hell, I followed her here!"

I said helplessly, "Mike—"

"Shut up and pull your gun!"

178

And then I heard Sue's voice. "Daddy, you can't! Mart hasn't done anything. He didn't bring me here, I came of my own free will. I thought— I wanted him to marry me but doggone him, he . . ."

She was beside me, her arms around me as though to keep me from drawing my gun. But her face was turned toward Mike.

In the yard there was only silence.

It was an instant before I comprehended her strategy. It was dark. Chances were Mike had never got close enough to Laura to see her clearly. To him, the one he followed had only been a woman and now he was beginning to wonder if he had not been a blind and jealous fool.

Sue cried, "I don't see why you had to come storming in here like this and threatening to shoot it out with Mart. You've always let me come and go as I pleased before. I'll make him marry me but you've got to give a girl a little time. I don't need any help from you!"

Mike said, "Mart, I— Jesus, why didn't you tell me it was Sue?"

I didn't say anything. I couldn't. I was glad it was dark so that he couldn't see the way I was grinning. Laura had been smart, but not quite smart enough. She hadn't counted on Sue.

Mike said, "You coming home, Sue?"

"I am not! What's this all about, anyway. First you're going to kill Mart because I'm here with him and then sudddenly you don't care. I—"

179

I squeezed her arm and whispered, "Don't lay it on too thick. Let him go."

Apparently Mike didn't know anything about the arrest of Swope and the four Fleur de Lis hands or about Father being hurt. And I didn't think this was the time to enlighten him. Laura might come to at any time and no telling what she'd do if Mike was still here when she did.

He swung to the back of his horse. He cleared his throat and started to say something, then changed his mind and rode out of the courtyard to the street.

I discovered that I was sweating and that my knees were trembling with relief. I said, "Now what do we do with her?"

"She's going to the stage depot. There's a stage out at five and she's going to be on it." She went inside, took the dipper out of the bucket beside the stove and flung the contents straight into Laura's face.

Laura gasped, opened her eyes and looked at us. She began to whimper. Sue said coldly, "That's not going to get you any sympathy. There's a stage out of here at five and you're going to be on it. Your little plan to get Mike killed didn't work. I convinced him it was me with Mart. But tomorrow, after he's cooled off a little, I'm going to tell him the truth."

She turned to me. "Help me get her up."

I picked Laura up. Sue held the door open and I carried her outside. I put her down on her feet and Sue closed the door, then took Laura's other arm. Supporting her between us, we walked out to the street and across the square to the stage depot. We took her inside, sat her down on one of the benches. Sue gave her some money and she took it without a word. She looked bedraggled and beat but I knew that wherever she went she would make men want her and give her the things she wanted. One lamp was burning dimly in the stage depot and the only other passengers waiting were a Spanish woman and five or six sleeping children.

Outside again, I headed across the plaza toward the sheriff's office. As we walked I said, "We went out to Fleur de Lis and arrested Swope and four of the men that were out at Cactus Springs. Both Swope and Father were shot."

"Oh, Mart, is he hurt very bad?"

"Pretty bad."

We reached the office and went inside. I glanced first at Father, who seemed no better, then at Francisca, sitting beside him. "Any change?"

She shook her head gloomily. In her eyes I could see the fatalistic belief that he was going to die.

20

I did not need to be told that morning would bring a showdown. Nor did I need to be told that I held an extremely poor hand.

A commotion might easily cause my father's death. If the cowmen tried to force the jail, as they surely would . . . I glanced at Sue. "You go home."

"I will not!"

181

"Then go to the hotel. If you see Mike, try and talk some sense into him."

"I'm not gong anyplace. I'm staying right here. I love you, Mart, and if there's going to be trouble—"

"If there's going to be trouble, your being here will only make it worse."

She shook her head stubbornly. I grabbed her arm and hustled her out the door. "Then I'll drag you to the hotel."

She tried struggling for a few moments, then gave it up. After that she walked meekly beside me, but I did not let go of her arm.

The air held the gray chill peculiar to the predawn hours. Light was beginning to show above the eastern horizon and it silhouetted the low adobe buildings of the town against the sky. Standing out above all the rest were the twin square towers of the church.

I was thinking that by his action last night, Father had removed from the sheriff's office all taint of partisanship. No longer could the homesteaders accuse him of closing his eyes to the things being done to them. But Father was flat on his back. And if the cowmen succeeded in breaking the prisoners out of jail . . .

I shouldn't have left the place at all, I thought. It was getting too close to dawn, to the time when the men from the ranches would hit the jail if they hit it at all.

We reached the hotel, but before I could take Sue inside, sound from the direction of the plaza reached my ears.

In the still dawn air, it carried perfectly. It was the rattle of many hoofs on the hard-packed streets. It was the sound of many horsemen riding through the town.

I released Sue. "Stay here! For God's sake, don't give me any argument now. I should never have left at all."

I began to run toward the jail. Anger boiled in me, but combining with it was a feeling of frustration and hopelessness. Even had I stayed at the jail I could not have prevented this from happening. I could not have waged a fight to retain the prisoners without endangering my father's life. No. Whatever fight I made would have to be made someplace besides the jail.

I increased my speed and began to grow short of breath. Damn it, if I was going to hold this job down very long, there would be some changes made. For one thing, I'd keep a horse tied at the rail out front so I wouldn't always have to be afoot.

It seemed like a mile through the twisting streets between the hotel and the jail. Most of the sky was still cold gray but above the eastern horizon there was the faintest show of pink.

I turned a corner and skidded to a halt. I was too late. I could see the square, and the jail, and the milling horses in the street before its door. Most of the riders had stayed in their saddles, but there were perhaps a dozen horses that were riderless.

And men were pouring out of the office door. In this light and at this distance, I could recognize only a few. I knew Swope by his walk and the white sling on his left arm. And I knew Montour.

I forced myself to remain still while my breathing quieted and became normal again. Seething, I watched them mount.

Most of them had been up all night, I guessed, for a good many of them were in various stages of drunkenness. One yelled, "The Diablo! Le's open it up an' get us all a drink!"

There was no dissent and the group whirled their horses and thundered across the square. I heard a tinkle of breaking glass at the Diablo and a few moments later saw the flicker of a lamp inside. The light rapidly increased as additional lamps were lighted.

I walked swiftly to the office and went inside. Francisca's face was white. Her hands were trembling, but she still sat where I had left her, at my father's side.

She gasped, "*Señor* Martin! They—"

I said, "I know. They took the prisoners." I looked at my father's face, noted the even rise and fall of his chest. "Is he all right?"

"Better, I think. His breath—it is easier."

Relief touched me and I nodded. I knew what I had to do. If I didn't do it, tomorrow would see a blood bath in this country worse than anything it had ever known before. The ranchers had deliberately flaunted and defied the law, and the significance of that would not escape the homesteader crowd. Tomorrow there would be open warfare in the streets of Rio de Oro. Unless I was successful in restoring order and recovering the prisoners.

I wasn't fool enough to believe I could do it. But there was a thin, small chance . . .

I found myself wondering what Father would have done, or rather how he would have done it, for there was little doubt in my mind that he would have done exactly what I now intended to do.

No deviousness in Father. He would have met the challenge head on, in the most direct way possible. Trouble was, I had neither his experience nor his reputation to make possible the task.

Lacking both experience and reputation, I would just have to use different tools. I went to the gun rack and got down the same shotgun I had used yesterday. From the drawer of the desk I got a box of shells and stuffed several handfuls into my pocket. Not that I was going to need more than two, I thought. I'd never get a chance to reload.

My hands were shaking and I wondered if his shook every time he loaded up a gun and went out of here. I supposed they had at first. Later maybe a man got so he could control that shaking or the outward evidence of it at least.

Yet I had watched my father go out after someone many times in my life and I doubted if he had ever been less than coldly sure of himself. I guessed I just wasn't cast in the same mold as he.

Francisca said frantically, "Martin! No!"

I glanced at her and scowled. "Stay right where you are. Look after him, no matter what happens. Understand?"

185

She nodded dumbly, the protest gone from her lips but not from her frightened eyes. I went out and closed the door.

I stared at the Diablo Saloon across the square. I was a fool to think I could walk in there, into that crowd of success-drunk cowhands, and take the prisoners back from them. I was a fool. Yet I knew that recapturing the prisoners was the one and only thing that could keep the peace in Rio de Oro today.

I clenched my jaws and started toward the saloon. I crossed the street and entered the square, my foot stirring the ashes of one of the homesteader's fires that had burned here yesterday. The sky in the east was lighter now, and the whole sky was washed with varying shades of violet and pink. The sun would be coming up soon.

By the time it did I would be either victorious or dead. I wondered what it was like to die, then angrily put the thought from my mind. The conflict existing here between homesteaders and cowmen no longer seemed important to me. Conflict had become a smaller issue and a personal one. I had a single job to do and I figured doing it successfully would put a stop to violence. But whether it did or not mattered less to me just then than the success of the job itself.

I thought briefly of Sue, then resolutely put thought of her away from me too. Nothing personal should enter my mind. I had to be a machine, intent on a single thing. Right now I was going after five prisoners. I was going to bring them back either dead or alive. I was going to try and stay alive myself until it was done.

The distance across the square seemed like a hundred miles. I reached the edge of the square and crossed the street to the gallery of the Diablo. The glass had been broken and someone had reached inside to unlock the door. There were probably half a dozen lamps burning. Tobacco smoke was already a pall in the air of the place.

I stopped for an instant just outside the door. Inside they were shouting and laughing and planning what they would do to the homesteaders when the sun came up. All I could think was that for this my father was lying near to death.

The slow, smoldering anger in me began to grow. It mounted like a forest fire leaping to crown the trees. Suddenly I was neither nervous nor afraid. I was just plain mad.

I kicked open the saloon door and stepped inside. Shifting the shotgun to my left hand, I snatched out my revolver and put three shots into the backbar. The mirror shattered and so did half a dozen bottles.

I doubt if anything could have startled them more. Immediately following my three shots there was complete silence in the saloon. Every man seemed frozen, staring toward me with pure amazement.

I holstered the revolver and shifted the shotgun. I thumbed back both hammers. I wasn't thinking very clearly but I remember hoping to God my voice came out right, strong and steady, not shaking and high.

I yelled furiously, "God damn you, all of you! Do you think he got himself all shot up for nothing? I want Swope and I want the other four that were in the jail. For good measure I want Montour for jail-breaking and I want you, and you, for setting fire to Satterlee's barn!"

I hadn't meant to go so far. But I knew Montour had been behind the jailbreak. And I recognized the other two from out at Cactus Springs.

I was watching Swope because I knew that whatever happened would start with him. No one moved. No one spoke. Nothing happened.

I bawled, "Swope! Damn you, move!"

He moved, slowly and deliberately. He turned his body from the bar and took an even step away from it. His feet were apart, his weight slightly forward. His right hand was suspended, away from his body, about six inches from the grip of his holstered gun.

I said coldly, "Don't touch it, you bastard! If you do, I'll blow you in two!"

The shotgun wasn't pointed directly at him. I wondered if I could drop its barrel in line and fire before he drew and fired at me. Apparently he was wondering the same thing, for I could see the calculation in his eyes. He was also hurting from the wound and feeling mean because he did. I could see that too.

I learned something in the next lightning instant. I had been watching Swope's eyes and they telegraphed his intentions to me by the slightest narrowing of the lids. He meant to draw and would in the next bare fraction of a second.

I didn't wait. I dropped the muzzle of the shotgun into line and fired.

Before the smoke of the blast obscured my sight of him, I saw his own gun come like a shaft of light from its holster. I saw it come level and saw flame spit from its muzzle. I felt something strike me in the thigh.

The leg gave beneath me and I staggered aside. But I caught myself and stood watching Swope double forward and fall on the dirty floor of the saloon.

He was almost cut in two. His midsection was a welter of blood. He was dead before he struck the floor, his eyes dull and without the spark that life puts into them.

There was a certain amount of hysteria in my voice that I simply could not control. I shouted, "Pick him up! Take him over to the jail! Reilly! Shane! Move!"

Nobody moved. I swung the gun toward Reilly and Shane, standing together down the bar a ways from where Swope had been. "There's a barrel left," I said.

They moved at last. They picked up Swope and started toward me with him. I said, "Montour— Dugan—LeBlanc—you other two—get going. The rest of you get your horses and go home. If I see any of you in town fifteen minutes from now . . ."

Montour shuffled toward me, his face nearly purple with rage. The others followed reluctantly. I backed to the wall on one side of the door. I looked straight at Montour and said, "Go ahead. Try it. But before you do, take a look at what this shotgun did to your son-in-law. If anything happens between here and the jail, you're the one I'm going to cut in two!"

His face lost color and he didn't look around. He muttered. "Take it easy, Mart. Take it easy. We're going."

His words seemed to ease the tension in the room. I waited until Montour and the others had gone out, until Reilly and Shane, both a little green from the sight of Swope, went out. Then I ducked out after them.

I half expected to see some of them trying to reach their horses, and was ready to shoot. But instead they were meekly trooping across the street toward the open plaza between the saloon and the jail.

I had won, damn it! I had won! I followed them across the square, across the street beyond to the door of the jail. Behind me there were subdued voices, but no shouts.

Montour went in first, followed by LeBlanc, Dugan and the other two. Reilly and Shane had fallen behind because of their burden. I said, "Lay him on the gallery. Then get inside."

They did. I went in, followed them back to the cells in the rear and locked them in. I returned to the office, clanging the door shut behind me. This time I put the cell keys into my pocket.

I glanced at my father and discovered that his eyes were open, watching me. I knew I was going to have a case of the shakes so I went outside.

Across the square a subdued and virtually silent crowd of punchers were mounting their horses and starting to leave town. I began to shake violently and for the first time I felt the pain of the bullet wound in my leg. I realized that I was soaked with sweat.

But I felt good. I felt strong, and alive, and I didn't need anyone to tell me that I was no longer "the sheriff's kid." I could see the proof of that in the subdued column of horsemen leaving town. I had seen it briefly in my father's open eyes just a few moments before. I saw it in Sue's shining face as she came running toward me from where she had been standing all this time beside a bench at the corner of the square.

I waited because I wasn't sure I could walk steadily on my injured leg. I broke the shotgun, took out the empty and the unspent shell, then leaned the gun against the adobe wall. My arms were waiting for Sue when she reached me and I put them around her and held her close to me.

It wasn't over. But between us, Father and I had put the law on top where it belonged. And peace would come to the country again because we had.

Center Point Publishing
600 Brooks Road • PO Box 1
Thorndike ME 04986-0001 USA

(207) 568-3717

US & Canada:
1 800 929-9108